HER WRANGLER WOLF

WILD FRONTIER SHIFTERS

MEG RIPLEY

SHIFTER NATION

CONTENTS

HER WRANGLER WOLF

HER WRANGLER WOLF

WILD FRONTIER SHIFTERS

1

"I SWEAR I CAN ALREADY SMELL THE FUNNEL CAKES and cigarette butts," Bryce observed as he stood at the edge of the fairgrounds. Right now, the place didn't look like much. It was a mostly flat field that surrounded a large arena and the grandstands. That was about it aside from a few other fenced-in areas, but it would change soon enough. Trucks pulling campers and horse trailers were already heading in. Workers were setting up food trucks and merchandise stands, and two others were stringing long lines of colorful flags from every light pole and fence. There were always a lot of tourists in town, but Bryce's keen senses easily picked up on the massive influx of more strangers. The rodeo was one of the biggest events in Sheridan, and the whole world seemed to know it.

Cash nodded. "It's going to be a lot to manage, and of course, the sheriff's department has a big involvement. I appreciate the two of you coming out to help set up."

Wade, Cash's former roping partner, braced his hands on his hips and shook his head. "I don't know how much I'll be able to do. Sierra and I have a lot going on already since we'll be competing, but I'll do whatever I can."

"I appreciate it," Cash said with a nod. "There's been quite the round of food poisoning in the city workers, so we're short."

"Looks like the entertainment has already shown up," Bryce commented as a massive tour bus pulled into the fairgrounds. It slowed down, hesitating as the driver tried to figure out where they were supposed to park. A young man wearing a reflective vest and carrying a couple of bright flags trotted forward to wave it into a spot at the edge of the parking area, near a thick stand of trees. "Who's the hotshot this year?"

"I haven't heard," Cash admitted. "I think the lineup changed a few times, and I'm not sure who finally ended up as the headliner. I've been too busy with the baby to worry about a damn concert."

"Guess we'll find out." Bryce leaned against a nearby fence as the bus's door opened. He was ready to make fun of whatever rhinestone cowboy might come out, hitching up his big buckle when he'd never even laid a hand on a horse.

Instead, a little boy descended the steps. He was geared out from head to foot like a rodeo star, with a hat that was slightly too big for him and fell over his eyes as he made the jump off the final step. He held a toy lasso and swung it wildly around his head as he pranced on the grass, pretending to ride a horse. "Woo hoo!" The rope flung against the side of the bus and flopped on the grass as the boy cheered himself on. He quickly picked the lasso back up and tossed it in the other direction. "Ride 'em, cowboy!"

A moment later, a woman came charging down the bus steps. Bryce froze as he took in her waves of pale auburn hair rippled with blonde and a very familiar set of dark eyes. He knew there was a 24-karat smile hidden behind her lips that were currently set firmly as she scooped the little boy into her arms. "Kipp! Don't run off like that! You scared me!"

She was just about to turn back for the bus when

her eyes lifted and met Bryce's, like a string stretched out between the two of them and had finally become taut. She hesitated for a moment and then carried the boy back onto the bus.

"I can't think of her name, but I'm pretty sure I saw her latest video the other day. Doesn't she sing that one about the horse?" Cash asked.

"Dakota fucking Jones," Bryce said quietly. His eyes were still locked on her as she stood in the bus doorway with her back to the world.

"Yeah, that's the one. That should be a good show. I think the kids' events are the first on the list. Let's go see what we can do to get that set up," the deputy suggested.

That was exactly why Bryce had come out there, but his wolf told him there was something far more important he needed to do at the moment. He had some old business to take care of, or maybe even rekindle for a night or two. "You two go on ahead and I'll meet you over there."

The other two eyed him warily, but they nodded and moved off. Everyone knew Bryce was a lone wolf who did things his own way, and there wasn't much point in trying to dissuade him.

When they were out of earshot, Bryce began making his way toward the tour bus. He automatically sidestepped around the other vehicles that were pulling in, barely even looking at them as his eyes were locked on Dakota.

As though she knew he was there, Dakota slowly turned. Her lips tightened slightly, and a crease appeared on her forehead as she came back down the bus steps and shut the door behind her. She threw her shoulders back and put her chin in the air as she approached him.

"You don't have to look like you're sacrificing yourself just to come talk to me," Bryce remarked as they met on a flattened area of grass. Dust swirled around his boots and lifted into the air. "As far as I recall, our last encounter was quite memorable."

"It was." She ran a hand through her hair and glanced over her shoulder.

Bryce's wolf was going nuts being this close to her. How long had it been? Five years? He could still remember that night of passion with complete clarity, though. "I'm pretty busy this week, but I'm sure I can find some time for you."

Dakota folded her arms in front of her, making her shirt strain against her breasts. She quickly readjusted her arms, tucking them this way and that as though she didn't quite know what to do with them.

She flapped one hand in the air, looking frustrated. "Things are different now."

Shit. Maybe that night hadn't been memorable in the way he'd hoped.

He looked up at the massive bus behind her. It was a far cry from the overpacked van she'd had the last time she'd come through Sheridan. "Yeah. You're a star now."

"I guess you could say that." She was looking everywhere but at him.

"And you've got a kid now," he noted.

Her tongue worked over the inside of her lips as she nodded.

The tension was thick between them. Bryce wanted to shove it out of the way. He was tempted to wrap his arm around her waist, pull her close, and remind her of just how much fun they'd had. But that obviously wasn't what she wanted. Damn.

"I've got things to do, Bryce. I'll see you around." She turned and quickly headed back to the bus.

Bryce knew she didn't mean that last part, but he was damned sure going to try to make it happen anyway. He barely paid attention to where he was going as he headed back over to the kids' area to join Cash and Wade, nearly stepping out in front of a truck on the way. The driver honked the horn at him, irritated, but Bryce just moved on through.

"Find what you needed?" Wade asked, sliding a meaningful glance over at Cash as they set up a series of pipe gates that would form a small corral for part of the petting zoo.

Bryce felt one corner of his mouth lift in something that was a bit too close to a smile, but he didn't bother forcing it back down. It was impossible not to remember those few nights with Dakota, back when she didn't have a big fancy tour bus or a care in the world. With a little bit of luck, he just might find a way to get her to remember how much fun they'd had. Maybe it wouldn't be so bad if he stuck around the fairgrounds and worked the rodeo a bit. He picked up the next piece of fencing and set it in place. "Yep. I think I did."

2

DAKOTA STOMPED BACK UP THE BUS STAIRS. SHE'D known there was a chance of running into Bryce there, but she'd hoped it was a slim one. The odds for this particular leg of her tour going smoothly seemed to be against her favor at the moment. No sooner did they roll into Sheridan, and there he was.

Of course, he still looked just as hot. Dakota wouldn't have ever admitted to anyone that she went for the bad boy type. And really, when it came down to it, she didn't. It was just that Bryce could pull it off so well. That shaved head and all those tattoos made him look like the kind of guy you wouldn't want to meet in a dark alley, and they were quite the contrast to his cowboy boots and tight jeans. You just didn't meet guys like Bryce anywhere, not even on the road.

"Mommy! Mommy, look! I'm a wolf! Awooo!" Kipp was on all fours now, barreling down the middle of the tour bus. Every now and then, he'd put his hands up on top of his head with his fingers together, pretending he had big wolf ears.

Frankie stepped out from the bathroom. Her denim button-down was spangled with sequins along the shoulders and down the sleeves, and large turquoise earrings dangled from each lobe. "I thought you were a cowboy now instead of a wolf," she said as her grandson clumped through the narrow hallway toward the back of the bus."

Dakota pursed her lips and sighed. "So much for having outgrown that phase. I thought he was all about cowboys. At least it's cheaper when he's into wolves. It means he's not constantly asking for a new pair of boots. Or those chaps with all the fringe off the back." She smiled a little at the thought, but her stomach was still in a thick knot after her encounter with Bryce. Dakota reminded herself that it was a brief run-in, and Sheridan was bound to be packed with people there for the rodeo. There was no guarantee that she'd see him again.

"Like you need to worry about money," came her

mother's sassy reply as she opened the door of the beeping microwave. "Hey there, wolfie! What do wolves eat for lunch?"

Only silence came from the back of the bus for a moment. "Uh, sheep?"

"Then come get your sheep dog while it's hot!" She put the hotdog on a bun, added a squirt of ketchup, and placed some chips on the side.

Kipp came charging back down the center of the bus and leaped up into the seat at the table. His feet were pulled up underneath him as he crouched in his best imitation of a wolf.

Frankie put out a finger just as Kipp bent his head toward his plate, preparing to take a bite of the hotdog without even picking it up. "Uh uh. Even wolves know how to be gentlemen sometimes. They know how to put their feet on the floor and use their paws."

A spark of defiance shone in Kipp's eyes, but he obliged and sat properly in his seat. "Sheep are really good," he said as he munched away.

Dakota shook her head. "I don't know what I'd ever do without you, Mom." She'd felt horribly guilty when her pregnancy had made her realize that she wouldn't be able to have a career without someone to watch Kipp. She hadn't liked the idea of just hiring anyone, no matter how good of a resume and references they might have. Fortunately, Frankie had been more than willing to jump in.

"Like I could just sit at home and knit while I waited for my daughter and my wild little grandson to come home and visit," Frankie said with a wink. She glanced at her reflection in one of the tinted windows and fussed with her hair, which she'd dyed a dark brown this time. "Should we get out and explore the place a little once he's done with lunch?"

"Maybe later. I've got a phone call to make." Dakota moved to the very back of the bus, which was entirely taken up by her bedroom. Not that Frankie and Kipp didn't both come in all the time, sprawling out on the bed to watch movies when they had time or nap on the comfortable mattress. It was close quarters on a tour bus, and Dakota was grateful that she got to share it with people she loved. Right now, though, she needed privacy.

"I need to speak to Ray, please," she said when the secretary answered the phone. "This is Dakota."

"Just a moment, please."

She puffed air into her cheeks and out her mouth, nervously pacing the small amount of floor-space as she looked out the window. There were now so many other vehicles surrounding theirs that she wasn't sure how Tyler would manage to maneuver the bus back off the fairgrounds once she gave him the go-ahead. Not wanting to think about it, she studied her nails. She hadn't bothered with a manicure in a while. It was such a pain to always have the polish chip as soon as she picked up her guitar. But she had to look good for the stage, of course.

"Dakota! My star!" Ray's voice burst through the phone, making Dakota pull it away from her ear for a moment. "Glad to hear from you. I was just thinking about you. I just got off the phone with the booking agent, and I've got the entire rest of your tour scheduled."

Pressing a hand against her forehead, Dakota forced herself to ignore that part. She wasn't ready to think about the future. She was focused on this week and her time in Sheridan. "That's great, but I need to talk to you about my next show. I want out of the Sheridan Rodeo."

Laughter came through the line, but it died off as soon as Ray realized she wasn't joking. "Dakota. Honey. You know that's crazy, right?"

"There's nothing saying I have to do this show. They can grab someone else. Lord knows there are plenty of country artists salivating at the chance to play a venue like this." She mentally reached out for some good excuse, something Ray would actually buy. She couldn't possibly explain the real reason. "I mean, don't you think I'm a little above this rodeo? I've sold out entire arenas."

"Sure, babe, but just think of PR you can get from a gig like this. You were small-time when you rolled through Sheridan a few years ago. Hardly any radio play, not a single music video. You weren't much more than a busker at that point, and the Sheridan Rodeo was your ticket to the big-time. That crowd ate you up and demanded seconds. You'd be nothing if it hadn't been for that show and how much of yourself you'd put into it."

Dakota bit her lip. The last five years had gone quickly. Her van had been replaced by this tour bus that cost more than most people paid for a permanent home. For her first gigs, she'd brought along an old friend as an impromptu bodyguard, not because she'd needed one, but because she was a little scared. Now he'd gone off to coach their high school's football team, and she'd hired Tyler from a security agency. Instead of long days with nothing to do but work on her music, she was constantly being shuffled from one venue to the next, herded quickly away from one event as soon as it ended to get to the next

one. Ray was right in so many ways, but he just
didn't get it.

"Yeah, but—"

"No buts, sugar. This is the show that made you.
This is you returning to your roots, if you will, and
it's been promoted that way. If you check your social
media accounts, you'll see that the fans are already
lapping it up like kittens on warm milk. You can't
even imagine the backlash you'd get if you canceled,
not to mention how much money you'd lose. This
isn't negotiable, Dakota." Ray's voice was usually
bright and cheerful. He often reminded her of a
used car salesman, one of those guys who did
horrible commercials for local television. But it
hardened on those last few words, and she knew he
was serious.

"Okay," she sighed. After all, he was the one
who'd helped make her into what she was. Dakota
had learned that it wasn't a simple matter of good
music, and she loved the fact that she could make
money doing what she was passionate about. "I'll
do it."

"That's my girl!" Ray boomed over the phone.
"I'll email you the rest of the schedule, and I'll make
sure Tyler has it as well. There are a few other

details I'm hammering out, so I'll get back to you on those. Need anything else?"

She shook her head, even though he couldn't see her. Dakota had known this was exactly how the phone call would turn out, but it was still disappointing. "No. I think I'm good."

"All right. You get out there and shine, Dakota! I'll talk to you soon!" The phone clicked as he hung up.

Dakota flopped backward on the bed. The luxurious comforter and the expensive mattress underneath her felt incredible, but they didn't make her feel any better. She just couldn't do this. Ray thought the Sheridan show was important, but he had no idea just how much of an impact it had made on her life. And that didn't have anything to do with her career. Her stomach swirled. She knew she should probably eat something, but she wasn't sure if she could.

A quiet knock sounded on the door.

"Come in."

The pocket door slid aside to reveal Tyler. His frame took up the entire narrow doorway and then some. His dark hair was buzzed short, with just a little more length on top. He'd never struck Dakota as a particularly fussy man, and it wasn't as though he spent a ton of time in the bathroom, yet he never had a hair out of place. At first, she'd thought he was nearly expressionless. Dakota rarely saw the bodyguard smile or even frown. But she saw a hint of something in those dark eyes of his that had her immediately sitting up again.

"What is it?"

He turned sideways to fit his massive shoulders through the doorway. He held something pinched between his index and middle finger. "Looks like we got another message from your friend."

It was a piece of paper, and as Dakota tipped her head to look at it, she realized it was the brochure for the rodeo. One page featured the details of the concert she was about to give in a few days, and someone had written just below her photograph in permanent marker. Dakota reached out to grab the brochure so she could read the scribbled handwriting.

Tyler immediately yanked it away. "You know better than that," he growled.

"You're such an ogre," she grumbled back, but she knew he was right. Dakota hadn't been entirely certain about Tyler when he'd first come onboard, but it was clear that he took his job very seriously. If there was anything on this piece of paper that could be harmful, then he wasn't going to take even the slightest risk that it would get to her. "You get to touch it."

"That's different." That was always his excuse.

Resigned, Dakota kept her hands to herself and tipped her head a little more as she read it. *I can't wait to see you, my love. You're going to be great.* The handwriting was, unfortunately, familiar.

If her stomach had already been upset at the idea of being in Sheridan, then she didn't quite know how to describe the feeling that this note gave her. "I didn't think he'd follow me here. He's always been in all the big cities, but this is a tiny venue compared to what I usually do."

Tyler nodded as he slipped the brochure into a Ziploc bag. For all she knew, he was going to have it analyzed for fingerprints, anthrax, or any number of things. "Keep in mind that all your tour dates are posted on your website. You can't expect any privacy when you're constantly promoting your location."

"Stop making it sound like it's my fault." Dakota grabbed a throw pillow off the bed and hugged it to her chest. "What the hell does this guy want from me?"

"I wouldn't bother trying to understand it. I just thought you should know."

"Thanks, I guess." This stalker of hers had been following her around for quite some time now. If she was frank with herself, Dakota had thought it was exciting at first. It meant she was famous enough for someone to become obsessed with her. Tyler had quickly put her in check, pointing out just how dangerous this sort of thing could be.

"Of course." Tyler shouldered his way through the door, his heavy footfalls thundering as he moved toward the front of the bus.

Pulling her knees up and bracing her heels against the bedrails, Dakota sighed. She could see the carnival being set up not too far away on the fair-grounds. It wasn't all that long ago that she would have split her time building up to the concert to both work on her music and to get out and have fun. That wasn't going to happen now, especially not if *he* was out there. Of course, heading out into Sheridan would also increase her chances of running into Bryce yet again, and she wasn't interested in that, either.

3

Bryce lay in bed, staring at the ceiling. Just as his alarm went off, the first rays of golden daylight began peering through the darkness of the room. He might have appreciated it if he hadn't already been awake for hours.

Slamming one hand on his alarm clock to shut it the hell up, he rolled out of bed. It was still a bit of a shock to find sleek hardwood floors under his feet instead of the ratty carpet of his old apartment. Colton had been on one hell of a streak of improving the Ward Ranch lately. Bryce wasn't sure if he was doing it because he wanted to impress his parents and remind them they'd made the right decision in leaving the place to him, or if it was simply because he wanted to show off in front of his mate. Willa was just as dedicated of a rancher, though, so maybe it was both.

Whatever. It didn't really matter. It was just nice to have a bunkhouse where he could crash without having to drive through the morning traffic to work. He mostly appreciated it, but today his thoughts were only on Dakota as he stumbled for the shower.

Holy hell. How long had it been? He scrubbed his scalp with his rough fingertips, his body on autopilot as all those memories came flooding back to him with unbelievable clarity. The days on the ranch could easily blur into each other, since so many of them were the same, but his brief time with Dakota was like another lifetime that he'd pushed to the furthest depths of his mind.

His wolf had tugged at him from the very first moment he'd laid eyes on her. Bryce had known instantly that this wasn't just some girl. This was the other part of his soul, the mate that his inner wolf had been searching for his entire life. Of course, he hadn't been interested in any long-term commitments, but he was fine with listening to those instincts as long as it meant he got to touch her long, cool fingers and look into those deep walnut eyes. He could ignore the rest of the implications behind that pull that constantly tugged at him.

After all, just because his soul was looking for a mate didn't mean he was ready for one. And Dakota was obviously human. He didn't even care that other shifters had made that work out. It was a ready excuse for keeping things short and uncomplicated.

Toweling off his tattooed body, he wondered if he could once again find a way to keep things simple and fun between the two of them. She'd have to be in Sheridan for about a week, given when the concert was, so he had a little time to work on it. He grinned to himself as he wrapped the towel around his waist and stepped out of the bathroom.

"You're in a good mood this morning," Caleb noted as he launched himself up off the couch with a towel in his hand and smacked Bryce on the shoulder. "Guess you had a good time in the shower?"

"Kiss my ass." Bryce wiped the grin off his face, not quite realizing that he was still smiling until Caleb pointed it out. This was his business, and he didn't want to talk about it in front of everyone else. No one would believe him anyway if he told them he'd seen every inch of the famous Dakota Jones. He glanced around the common room at the center of the big bunkhouse. "Isn't Zane up yet?"

Caleb shrugged as he stepped into the bathroom.

"I think I heard him rattling around in there. You know how he is."

Yeah, Bryce did. He wasn't sure that he cared for Zane all that much. Someone who was even more of a lone wolf than himself had to be one hell of an oddball. As much as Bryce thought he kept to himself, Zane was even more closed off. He'd never shared much information about his family or his background, even if they went down to the Full Moon Saloon and had a few beers. Bryce suspected that Colton had hired him purely for his background in construction, because it served his needs for upgrading the ranch.

Throwing on his typical work uniform of jeans, boots, and a white t-shirt, Bryce was just about ready for the day. He kept his head shaved, so other than an appointment with a razor a couple of times a week, he didn't have to worry about his hair. He headed toward the fridge, figuring on a bowl of cereal before he started his day just as Zane came out of his room. "Morning."

"Morning." Zane shut his door and kept his distance in the small kitchen as he fried two eggs and slid two pieces of bread in the toaster.

"You went to bed a bit early last night. Did you

hear that we're supposed to have a meeting this morning?"

Zane's bright green eyes darted to him. "A meeting? More improvements, maybe?"

Bryce shrugged. "Don't ask me what it's about. I don't have a clue. I'm just ready to get the day started." He sat down with his bowl of Mini Wheats, thinking that a day in the saddle would be just what he needed until he came up with some sort of plan.

Because there had to be a plan in place if he was going to have any chance at finding time with Dakota. She wasn't the same person she'd been the last time she'd rolled through Sheridan, not really. She was a celebrity now. There were probably all sorts of people constantly trying to get pictures or autographs, and that meant she likely had security. Plus, there was the fact that she had a reputation to keep up with. Everyone knew her for being pretty clean. There were never any overdose and rehab stories or sex tapes in the entertainment columns about her. She was just a singer who could afford a more expensive guitar these days, and in all likelihood, she wasn't going to let some grubby, tattooed ranch hand come rock that tour bus for an afternoon.

And then there was the kid. That was bound to

make things more difficult. Her attitude toward Bryce the previous day had proven that.

Rinsing out his bowl, Bryce found that the grin of hope and excitement he'd had when he'd come out of the shower had now turned into a deep frown. Getting to Dakota wasn't going to be easy. At all.

A short while later, Bryce, Zane, and Caleb were assembled in the dining room of the main house. This was where Colton and his mate Willa lived, and where generations of Ward ranchers had lived before them once they'd moved out of the tiny home at the back of the property that was now used as a hunting cabin. Bryce had been working for the Wards for a long time, and they treated their workers like family. He settled in easily with a cup of coffee as he waited for the bosses to get started, figuring they'd probably want to go over what stud bull they'd be using this year or what new building they were planning for next.

Willa's blonde hair was captured in its usual thick braid that draped over her shoulder. The angle of her arm and Colton's suggested they were holding hands under the table, and her eyes were warm as she glanced at him. "Go ahead, honey. Tell them."

Colton leaned back in his chair and grinned. "We've decided to sponsor part of the kids' area at the rodeo this year. It turns out the folks who were supposed to be in charge of that had something come up, and that's left the rodeo short an attraction that pulls in a really big audience. With the animals that we have here, as well as a few we're going to borrow from our neighbors, we'll be running the pony rides and the petting zoo."

Bryce felt his eyebrows meet in the middle of his forehead. Many things had changed at the Ward Ranch since Willa had come aboard, so he wouldn't have been surprised by almost any announcement that came across the table. This, though, wasn't anything like he'd imagined. "What?"

Willa's smile grew as she gave another loving glance toward her mate. "We're all going to take turns running it, so the shifts shouldn't be too long. Of course, we'll pay for the extra hours put in. I know it's a bit of a surprise, but we feel this is really important to Sheridan as well as to the ranch. We want to do everything we can to help."

"It's kind of bad timing for me," Zane said in that raspy voice of his. "I just got word this morning that my aunt is really sick. She's in the hospital, and I was actually going to ask for the day off to take care of her."

"Zane, I'm so sorry to hear that," Willa said sympathetically. "What's the matter with her?"

He lifted one shoulder. "They're still trying to figure that out, but I don't think things are looking all that good."

"Take the day and keep us posted," Colton said. "We'll manage."

Sure, they'd manage. How convenient of Zane to have a sick relative right before Colton and Willa asked them to put in extra hours. Bryce stared down into his coffee, thinking about what this would mean for him. He would be at the fairgrounds more often, which would put him closer to Dakota, but he wanted to be wining and dining her, not stuck with the rugrats. "Why are we the ones running this?" he asked. "What about the other ranches?"

"Everyone is contributing in different ways," Colton replied. "I know the Crawfords are helping out with the food, and of course, plenty of other folks we know are competing themselves. Everyone's pulling their weight to help make this a success. I'm sure I don't need to remind you how much the tourism from the rodeo helps Sheridan. I could always send you down to talk to Harper, but I'm not sure she'd have time for you right now."

Bryce rolled his eyes. Austin Crawford's mate was

a transplant from the city, and she was a perfect fit for the tourism board. Bryce had no doubt that what she did was important, but he didn't want a lecture on it. "No, that's okay."

"All right." Willa passed out a few sheets of paper. "This is the schedule I worked out to make sure the kids' area is covered. Zane, one of us will fill in for your shifts for the moment. Just let us know how things go."

His brilliant green eyes were appreciative as he nodded. "Thank you."

"And of course, some of our other, bigger projects around the ranch will be suspended while the rodeo is in town," Colton added. "They can wait for a little while, and then we'll get back to normal."

Everyone started to get up from the table to start the day. There was always plenty of work to be done around the ranch. Provided there weren't any cattle that needed vaccinations or medical care of some sort, there was always fence to repair or a pasture gate to be opened or closed. Bryce tipped back the last of his coffee and scrubbed his hand over the skim of fuzz on his head as he rinsed out his cup.

"Hey," Willa said, suddenly appearing next to him at the kitchen sink. "Are you okay?"

"I..." Bryce realized he'd just about told her. He'd

liked Willa right away, as soon as Colton had hired her as a ranch hand. Just like most of his kind, he'd been a bit leery about having a human come work on a ranch that'd been run by shifters for over a hundred years. She'd turned out to be one hell of a rancher and much easier to get along with than he'd anticipated. Still, he didn't think she'd appreciate his tale of cavorting with a country singer and trying to figure out how to get back into her bed. "I'm fine."

"Okay. You know I'm here if you need me." She refilled her mug with coffee, glanced at her mate, and left the kitchen.

Bryce felt his cheeks redden a little. He knew what they were doing. Colton and Willa were like the parents of their little ranch family now, even though Colton's parents came up from Florida every now and then. It was nice, but Bryce wasn't sure he wanted the attention.

Colton leaned against the counter and waited until the coast was clear. "You know it's going to drive her crazy if she thinks there's anything wrong," he said quietly.

Bryce let out a wry laugh. "Isn't there always something wrong?" he challenged. "You know what my life has been like."

"But it's not like that now," Colton pointed out.

"Sure, but that doesn't mean my past doesn't affect my present." Damn it. Bryce hadn't meant to talk about any of this. It was that bond with Dakota. It turned him into an idiot. He'd seen her for all of ten seconds and she'd already managed to break through the walls he'd so carefully built. Bryce hadn't even realized he'd been thinking this way until it'd come out.

"And what is it affecting right now?" Colton smoothed back his dark hair, shaved close at the sides and grown out longer at the top, before he filled his mug and grabbed an extra biscuit from the plate on top of the stove. "Want one?"

Bryce started to shake his head, but Willa did make some really good biscuits when she decided to cook. He grabbed one and took a bite, not bothering with any butter or jelly as he contemplated his dilemma with Dakota. "You and Willa work out really well, you know?"

"I do." Colton raised an eyebrow, waiting patiently for the rest of the story.

It was hard to figure out where to start. He didn't want to just come right out and tell Colton he'd found his mate, and he especially didn't want to say that she was not only a human, but a celebrity. It just sounded so ridiculous, even in his head. "I didn't have a good upbringing. You know that. My parents were both too busy with all the drugs they were dealing to pay any attention to me. When they did, it was usually just my dad beating the hell out of me."

Colton watched him carefully. "You've mentioned a little about that."

Bryce sighed. He wasn't trying to make this about his past, but it was hard not to. Bryce knew that he'd kept himself as independent as possible because that was the safest way to avoid the hurt and disappointment. Even being part of Shaw's pack wasn't always easy, and he hardly even participated. "It's just that I've been seeing you and Willa together. You came from good families, from parents who taught you how to make things work. I didn't have that, and I'm not sure I'd ever be ready to deal with that sort of commitment."

"I have a feeling that all of this isn't coming up just because you see the way Willa and I are. I know we don't hide our love for each other, but we're not exactly making out in front of everyone. Is there someone in your life?"

Damn him for being observant when Bryce was always trying to keep his emotional doors and windows closed. "Not necessarily. Think of it as more of a possibility, one that I'm not sure what to do with." His body was only concerned with getting Dakota in bed. His wolf was nagging at him, reminding him that there was a potential for much more than just sex. That meant commitment. It meant being solid and steady, ready to be there for someone, no matter what the situation was. It even meant letting someone get a real view of what was going on behind the scenes, and someone like Dakota was going to be shocked when she saw that not only was it not pretty, but that he wasn't just a simple human.

Colton polished off his biscuit and wiped his hands on his jeans. "Is this the sort of situation I think you might be talking about?" he asked suggestively. "A particularly strong bond, perhaps?"

"Don't make me more embarrassed than I already am," Bryce pleaded. He knew what he felt in his heart and soul. He'd known a long time ago. It was just one of those things that didn't make any sense. Even if he laid himself bare in front of Dakota and told him exactly how he felt about her, then what? How could a man whose life was devoted to a piece of land and a herd of cattle be a good partner to someone who was constantly on the road and in the spotlight? How could he possibly deal with that sort of commitment?

Crossing the room to the window, Colton looked out over the barn and part of the pastures. "You know, when I first hired Willa, I worried that it was a mistake. I acted on my instincts, and I questioned myself about a thousand times on whether I was being an idiot. I also wondered which head I was thinking with."

"Oh, I think I know which one it was," Bryce cracked.

His boss let the joke go. "My problem—and the problem you're having right now—is that you're trying to be logical about something to which logic doesn't even apply. You can't take all those feelings and instincts and force them to make sense, because they're never going to. That being said, I think these things usually work out the way they're supposed to."

"Maybe." Bryce contemplated that for a moment. He knew how much Colton had risked—and even how much the two of them had sacrificed—as he and Willa had sorted themselves out. Of course, they had both been dedicated to the ranch. They were somewhat ordinary people working ordinary jobs. It just felt like this problem with Dakota was so much heavier. "I'm not confident that it will."

"At least give it a shot," Colton advised. "I know

how you are, and I'm not about to try to make you give me all the details, but don't sell yourself short. You might be more ready for a mate than you realize."

"I don't know. It's not all up to me, either. She'd have to be a part of that decision, too." His stomach dropped down into his boots as he imagined coming to Dakota with such a huge revelation. Did humans have a clue what it meant to be destined for someone? He thought about asking Colton, given that his mate had once been a human, but he didn't want to give away too much.

Colton clapped him on the shoulder. "Give yourself more credit than that. We'd better get to work, especially with the extra shifts we'll be putting in due to the rodeo, but let me know how it goes."

"I will." Bryce liked Colton and considered him one of his best friends. That didn't mean he was going to come back and dish everything about whatever might or might not happen between himself and Dakota. He'd have to figure it out on his own.

4

THE ALARM CLANGED THROUGH DAKOTA'S HEAD. SHE blindly swept the nightstand for her phone, swiping at the screen. She rolled over and groaned. It'd been a long night. Being on the road always wore her out, yet it wasn't the kind of exhaustion that made it easy to just fall into bed and sleep all night. The tension in her shoulders reminded her of just how much she'd tossed and turned at the beginning of the night. Once she'd finally fallen asleep, she'd been haunted by dreams of this mysterious stalker. Her overtired mind had wandered through the fairgrounds, watching around every corner for someone to jump out and grab her. She'd called out for Tyler, sure that her stalker was hiding just behind a bit of fence or a horse trailer, but the bodyguard had been nowhere in sight. Dakota's body had been stiff with fear as she tried to find her way back to the tour bus.

Bryce had been in her dreams as well, but those dreams left her feeling completely different.

Blinking, Dakota reminded herself that no matter how frightening it had been in the moment, it was all just a dream. Rory Black had been identified by her security team several months ago, and he'd been banned from all of her shows. They'd decided not to press charges against him, considering that what he'd done amounted to a lot of emails and messages, comments on her social media pages, and buying a hell of a lot of tickets and merchandise. He wouldn't be able to get anywhere near her as long as Tyler was on the scene, and that was simply part of being a celebrity.

Rolling onto her stomach and stretching her toes, Dakota raised the blinds on the window above her bed to peek out over the fairgrounds. Most of her view was obstructed by the various campers and trailers that were set up nearby, even though her bus was separated from the rest. She wondered how excited the visitors must be. All the cotton candy, carnival rides, watching both the stars and the people they knew from school compete in the rodeo, getting to watch a big concert... It had to be a blast for them, and she wished she still knew how to experience life that way.

"Mommy!" Kipp came bursting in from the adjoining room in his Toy Story pajamas. He jumped up onto the bed and wrapped his little arms around her, his hair still smelling of his green apple shampoo from the night before. "What are we doing today?"

Her heart shattered, and not for the first time. Dakota had quickly discovered that being a mother meant getting her heart broken over and over as her son experienced the ups and downs of life. Mostly, she just felt incredibly guilty for always needing to work. She reasoned with herself that there were plenty of other working mothers on the planet, and at least Kipp got some amazing experiences by being on tour with her, but it usually didn't make her feel any better.

"Well, baby, I've got an interview with the local news station today. Then I have someone calling to interview me for a podcast over the phone." She clutched Kipp tightly to her as she glanced at her guitar on its stand in the corner of the room. What she really *wanted* to do was focus on writing music. Unfortunately, being a celebrity was all about the media circus, and that left precious little time for her actual craft.

"Can I come to your inta-voo?" he asked.

Dakota stroked her hands down his little back. "No, honey. Not this time. I'm sorry. I'm sure you and Grandma will find plenty of fun things to do today. There are some good cowboy stores here in Sheridan. Maybe you can go to one of those and get a new hat."

Kipp rolled off of her and flopped spread-eagle onto the mattress. "I don't need a new hat. I want to be a wolf."

Oh, boy. There he went again. It was much easier to dress a little cowboy than a wolf, especially when there was always a chance of someone taking a photo of him and criticizing her parenting skills. "Who knows? Maybe you can find a store that has some wolf ears or something. Let's get up and get some breakfast."

The day went by quickly. Dakota smiled for the camera, and she put on her best voice for the podcast. She was fully aware that everyone was looking, watching, judging. The slightest flaw would be enough to set the internet on fire with comments. Dark circles under her eyes would make them think she wasn't sleeping, or if the Wyoming dust kicked up in her eyes and made them red, then she'd be on drugs. Too much weight, too little weight, too expensive of a shirt, too cheap of a guitar. She was fully in the spotlight, even when she wasn't on the stage.

Through it all, though, Bryce kept creeping into her mind. He was bad for her in so many ways, and her celebrity status was the least of it. Still, the constant schedule and the numerous reminders of just how distant she'd become from reality made her wonder how things might've turned out differently if she hadn't made it so big. Dakota would be completely free to go find Bryce or any other man and just hang out. Of course, no other man had quite affected her the way Bryce had. Those bad boy looks had sucked her in completely, from the dance of the colored lines over the long, corded muscles of his arms to the wild look in those light brown eyes. He was the sort of man who couldn't be tamed, the type who would never settle down and be happy working a nine-to-five job and coming home to help raise children. Dakota hadn't cared about any of that when she'd met him before.

She wasn't sure she cared about it right now as she remembered just how much fun he'd been. Bryce had known exactly how to handle her, bringing her skin to life with either the lightest touch against her throat or the strongest grip on her hips. He'd both owned her and set her free in those few nights they'd managed to spend together, slipping off to her van or a motel or even a field not far out of town. Bryce had been a complete stranger, and she had no reason to trust him or to give herself to him so willingly, yet she'd found that she didn't need a reason. Logic didn't have anything to do with it. Soon enough, she had to be on her way again, working the next leg of her meager tour to form the career she'd been dreaming of her entire life.

It was late when she'd finally gotten back to the tour bus. Frankie had cooked, as she often did, and she was keeping everything warm on the stove. "Dinner's ready, so I hope you're hungry."

"I know I am." Tyler eagerly dished up a loaded plate and sat down to shovel it in. The man seemed to appreciate the home-cooked meals just as much as any of them.

Frankie laughed and handed a plate to Dakota. "How about you, honey?"

She took the empty plate, but she held it limply in her hand as she eyed the food on the stove. "I don't know. I had a snack in the car."

"Come on, now. You need food. Kipp is already in bed, by the way. We took your suggestion and went shopping, and I wore him out. Check out these gorgeous earrings I bought, though." She tucked her hair behind her ears to show off the long dangles of hammered silver.

A pang of regret ripped through her chest at knowing she wasn't going to get to give Kipp a bath or even tuck him in. She hardly ever got to do what she wanted while she was touring. It was all about the fans. They paid the bills, for sure, but what about her? Shouldn't she have a chance at a little fun for herself? "Actually, I think I'm going out for a bit."

"Give me a second to finish this," Tyler grumbled as he scooped up a forkful of sweet potato.

"No, that's okay. This is something I need to do by myself. Just an errand I need to run while I'm here." It was dark out. She could take the car and maybe ask one of the locals how to find Bryce. What was the name of the ranch he worked on? What if he worked somewhere else at this point? Why had she been such a stubborn idiot when he'd shown up at her bus, strolling up not five minutes after they'd parked like fate had steered him right to her, and not asked him what he was up to these days?

Tyler moved his bulk uncomfortably in the booth seat at the table. "I don't like that."

"I know you don't," Dakota snapped back.

She'd apologize to him later, but it was about time she found a way to make this tour work for her, not just for everyone else. "I've got my phone. I'll be back in a bit." Charging back to the door, Dakota careened down the stairs and practically jumped off the last one onto the trampled grass waiting for her below. She held her jaw tight as she shut the door behind her, knowing she was throwing a fit like a child, but hardly caring. Dakota wanted to blow off some steam, and that was what she was going to do whether she found Bryce or not.

"Dakota."

She whirled around to find a pair of whiskey-colored eyes boring straight into her soul. Her heart hammered in her chest and adrenaline shot through her system, and she took a deep breath to calm them both.

"I didn't mean to startle you," Bryce said, lifting his chin and eyeing her carefully. "Are you all right?"

All right? Well, he hadn't been Rory Black, finally tracking her down just as he was trying to do in her nightmares. In that sense, yes. "I just thought you were someone else."

Something flashed through his eyes that she couldn't quite interpret, but it was gone in a moment.

"I was just coming to talk to you, if you have a minute."

Composing herself and glad to see that no one was around, she nodded. "Actually, I was just going to see if I could find you."

Bryce was keeping his distance, hovering a few feet away and staying out of the light that shone down from the kitchen window, like a wild animal that didn't want to be caught. He turned his head slightly to the side as he looked at her, which only magnified that feral look. "You were going to come find me when I could be anywhere in Sheridan or on the outskirts?"

Dakota rubbed her tongue against the inside of her lips, wondering for a brief moment if this was all just a mistake. "I never said it was a good idea."

"Most people don't think I am," he said matter-of-factly, taking a step forward. "Have you eaten?"

Her stomach rumbled in response for her. There was a plate of good, home-cooked food waiting for her, but she didn't care. It would just remind her of how trapped she was. "I haven't."

Without hesitation, Bryce grabbed her by the hand and began moving off across the fields, slipping between vehicles and winding around fences as though he could see in the dark. "I know it's probably not the fancy food you're used to, but I think I know where to get some corn dogs and funnel cakes. Or maybe some brisket and ribs, if you prefer."

Dakota felt a giggle bubble up in her throat as she trotted to keep up with him. She caught it in her teeth, not yet ready to let him know just how excited she was for this. "I'm not picky. I eat a lot more fast food than you might imagine."

"Yeah?" They stepped out into the main thoroughfare of the carnival, and he headed confidently to the area where most of the food trucks were gathered. "Then maybe things haven't changed as much as I thought."

"Probably not." She eyed his arms and back as he ordered for them. He'd filled out a little over the years, but definitely not in an unappealing way. His muscles bulged against the thin material of his shirt. His shoulders were wide and his arms strong, but every bit of him was also lean from long days in the saddle. The sun had deepened the color of his skin, yet his tattoos still popped out in the fluorescent lights that surrounded the food truck. Dakota was hungry all right, but she wasn't sure that food was what she was looking for.

"What are you grinning about?" he asked when their hands were full of corn dogs and lemon shake-ups and they headed over a small area full of picnic tables.

"You really want to know?" She sat on the bench, the scent of the fried food that surrounded them enticing her. A stomachache was likely on the menu by the time she was done there.

Bryce launched himself easily up off the bench so that he sat on the tabletop, his boots next to her. He loomed over her in that position, his eyes dancing in the odd light. "I wouldn't ask if I didn't."

She rolled her shoulder slightly. Dakota hadn't planned to tell Bryce much of anything, opting instead for a night of simple fun that wouldn't matter at all by the next morning. But what the hell? This was a night just for her, and she could say and do whatever she wanted. "I don't remember the last time someone else bought me dinner." A bolt of excitement shot through her tongue as she looked up at him.

His muscles were tense as he ate, like he was ready to spring up and jump into action at any moment. "So things *are* different."

"In some ways." Dakota wasn't sure why he was focusing so much on the changes that'd occurred since the last time she'd come to Sheridan, but she supposed she couldn't blame him. She wasn't just a girl with a guitar, hoping someone would bother slowing down to listen to her music. Not anymore.

Bryce gestured with his corn dog at the carnival, busy with adults and children alike moving from one attraction to the other with the lights reflecting in their eyes. "Think the media will have a heyday with that? Some random dirtbag buying you a cheap meal?" There was a light in his eyes, too, and she knew without question that it was a joke.

"I don't care, and I don't think you do, either. I haven't seen nearly as many cameras up here as I do in other places. Of course, I don't give them a lot of reason to come after me." If she kept her nose clean and there weren't any scandals to report, then what did they have to take photos of other than her buying a loaf of bread?

"They do anyway, though." Bryce chucked the stick from his corn dog into a fifty-gallon barrel that had been turned into a trash can. "I was curious after I saw you the other day. You're all over the place. They really like to get those shots of you with no makeup on."

Dakota felt her body pulling toward him. She obliged it to a degree as she pushed herself up onto the tabletop next to him. When was the last time someone had been so real with her? Bryce wasn't kissing her butt to get an interview or an autograph, nor was he handling her with kid gloves or fussing over her schedule. "Were you this much of an ass the last time?" she asked with a smile.

His eyes locked on hers, holding her in place with no more than a look. "Definitely."

She laughed as she leaned back on her arms. "How brave are you?"

"As brave as I need to be."

"Want to see if we can make ourselves puke on these rides?" Dakota leaped to the ground, pleased with the way the dust kicked up around her boots. She felt like a teenager again instead of an adult with a child and responsibilities.

"There's a short line at the Tilt-a-Whirl."

The ride operator did a double-take as they clambered through the gate and chose a seat. The ride started up and the force threw his long, hard body against hers. Dakota closed her eyes as the world spun around her, and they laughed together as they turned first in one direction and then the other. His arm closed around her waist to keep her from sliding toward the edge of the cart, and she leaned hard into him as they swooped downhill around the little ride. It was just kids' entertainment, but in the moment, it was even better than being on stage in front of a packed stadium.

Her vision swirled as the ride came to a halt, and she nearly fell over as she tried to stand. "Wow. I think it's been a little too long since I've done that."

Bryce was right there, holding her up as he led her toward the exit. He practically carried her down the short set of metal stairs, grabbing her by the waist when it was obvious she was far too dizzy to do it on her own. "You sure you're all right?"

Dakota lifted her head to say she was, but the motion was too much. She careened right into him, and he caught her in both arms. She was vaguely aware of the other riders streaming past them and moving on to the Ferris wheel or the carnival games, but once she'd managed to focus on the sweet bourbon of his eyes, the rest of the world disappeared. "Bryce, I..."

His dark brows dipped down in concern, and even though she'd gotten her footing, Dakota made no move to push herself off of him. It felt good, just standing there in his arms.

"What is it?" he asked, a hint of a smirk curling up the corner of his lips.

"I..." Her voice faltered once again as she studied his face. How could absolutely everything about him be so damn sexy? His jawline, the tendons in his throat as she looked up at him, the expression and spirit in his eyes that changed every time she looked at him. It would be so easy to unload all her secrets, to tell him the truth, to stop worrying about whether or not he would find out. Dakota pulled in a breath to try once again, but there was still that savage, untamed look in his eyes. She hadn't seen him in five years, and people could change a lot in that span of time. She certainly had, but not him. There was still so much chaos living inside Bryce.

"I'm just glad to see you again," she finally finished.

He let out a small laugh as he turned to the side so they could work their way through the rest of the carnival. "You're starting to make me think they put something strong in that lemon shake-up."

Dakota allowed herself to lean her head on his arm. She didn't have to tell him everything, and that would be good enough.

5

BRYCE FELT HIS WOLF HOWLING WITHIN HIM, AND IT was getting harder to control now that Dakota was so close to him. He'd come to the fairgrounds on the slim hope that he'd at least get a chance to talk to Dakota. He had very little hope that Colton's advice would be sound and that he'd actually find himself ready to become a full-time mate. He'd figured there was at least a chance that he could get shot down again. If he'd given her time to think and she still didn't want to have anything to do with him, then at least he'd know he tried.

Of course, it had all gone in a completely unexpected direction. The energy coming off of Dakota had been vibrant, maybe even angry, yet she'd been more than willing to come along with him for an impromptu dinner. Even then, as they'd chatted on the picnic table, he'd half-expected her to go flitting back to her tour bus once she realized what a mistake she'd made.

Now, she was strolling along at his side as though they'd been best friends all along.

It wasn't that he minded. Not at all. Just having the chance to be this close to her without her shooting daggers at him was more than he'd thought he'd get. She was a star, and she was well above him, even before she'd made it big. She probably hadn't grown up wondering where her next meal was going to come from or being told that she'd never amount to anything. His lupine side was over the moon, but it still felt surreal to his human side.

"What changed your mind?"

"Hm?" Dakota adjusted her grip on the little green teddy bear he'd won for her by knocking over some old glass bottles with a baseball.

The game was supposed to be rigged, but he'd learned a long time ago that there was a perfect way to throw the ball just right. The look on the carny's face was always worth it, even without the weird little teddy bear. "I was just wondering what made you change your mind. When I saw you the other day, you didn't want anything to do with me. I thought maybe it had something to do with Kipp's father."

Dakota's eyes widened for a moment before she looked away. "No. It's nothing like that. I was just surprised to see you after all this time, and I realized it would be nice to get out and have a little fun."

"But you're worried about someone seeing us together," he concluded as he watched her crank her head to the side to look at a young man with shaggy dark hair.

"Why do you say that?"

"The way you keep looking around. It's okay. I mean, I can understand why you wouldn't want anyone to see us together, especially if they're going to put it all over the tabloids. 'Country Star Steps Out with Rebel Ranch Hand' might not exactly be great for your career."

"Don't be ridiculous." She stopped as they passed a booth selling commemorative rodeo t-shirts and looked up at him. Dakota shoved her shoulders down as though she was forcing herself to relax. "It's not easy for me to be out in public, and I've probably got a few bad habits that are hard to break. It's nothing, though. I'm having a great time."

Her eyes drifted down to his lips and flicked back up to gaze into his eyes. Bryce's wolf thrashed inside him, and he felt the prickle of fur threatening on the underside of his skin. He'd been fighting to keep control of himself all evening. His animal self knew exactly what was going on, what bond the universe had created between them. It knew that this was bound to happen all along. The two of them were supposed to find a way to be together, no matter what she did for a living or how he felt about his past and his readiness for the future. His stomach tightened as he felt that same connection with her that he'd experienced before, the one that had both frightened and intrigued him more than anything he'd felt in his life. Bryce fell face-first into it as he bent his head to press his lips to hers.

She was soft and warm, tasting of lemons and sugar. The perfume that still clung to her neck lifted from her heated skin and turned his excitement up a notch as he brushed a hand through her soft hair. Dakota's body pressed against his as though she needed him to hold her up, but this time, he was the one who was dizzy. Adrenaline and emotions churned inside him as he felt the slightest part in her lips. Bryce slipped his tongue inside, eager to explore while she was willing to give him a chance.

Dakota's body pressed harder against his as her fingers gripped the cotton of his t-shirt. Her response nearly made him lose control. Blood surged to other parts of his body and left him dazed as he pulled back for a breath. When she looked up at him with her lips wet from his own and her eyes shining, he could see his own longing reflected in her face. Bryce knew he couldn't wait any longer.

He once again took her by the hand. This time, they weren't threading their way toward the lights and sounds of the carnival, but away from them. Bryce wasn't even entirely sure where he was heading, but his instincts drove him out to the field where he'd left his truck. He opened the door and helped Dakota up into the passenger seat before he trotted around to the other side, knowing only that they had to get away from the crowds, away from either of their lives, away from everything they knew.

It was a short drive out to a field near Black Tooth Park, the first place he could think of for the two of them to be alone. It was just a long enough drive to make him wonder if this was a good idea. He knew what was between them, but he also knew what differences they had. His wolf would be all the more distraught when she was gone once again, because Dakota had no reason to want to stay there with him.

When he threw the car in park and turned to

her, prepared to tell her he'd take her back to the carnival if she wanted him to, he didn't get a chance. She already had her seatbelt off and her arms around him, her lips trailing over his and down the side of his neck, her hands splayed against his chest and her body throbbing. When the tip of her tongue flicked the lobe of his ear, he threw the door open and his doubts out the window. "Come with me."

The bed of his truck was cool and quiet, and the vehicle rocked slightly as he held out his hand to help her up into it. They sank down on top of an old blanket he'd had in the cab, and Bryce was pleased to find that she was just as eager to be out there like a teenager as he was. Her hands gripped the hem of his shirt and lifted it in frustration, and once the garment was out of the way, she traced her fingers over the tattoos on his chest.

Bryce kicked off his boots and pulled at hers before his fingers reached for the tiny, delicate buttons on her shirt. He felt himself slipping out of control as he cupped his hands around her breasts and laved his tongue over her nipple, but he shoved his wolf back into place. She wouldn't touch him again if she knew what he really was.

Dakota's groan of pleasure echoed in his mouth as she flicked his belt buckle open and worked at his fly. Her hands slipped inside the waistband of his boxer briefs and closed around his cock, her fingers long and cool as she explored his length. He'd envisioned getting together with her again plenty of times, but none of those fantasies held a candle to the reality of it all. Dakota wanted him.

It was hard to concentrate on anything other than how good she was making him feel, but Bryce knew that he wanted to bring her just as much pleasure. He unbuttoned her jeans and shimmied them off her hips, taking a moment to let his hands enjoy the soft flesh of her backside. She parted her legs for him as he touched the insides of her thighs, and he could feel her heat radiating even before he touched her.

The muscles in her lower abdomen shivered in delight as he gently moved his fingers onto the delicate flesh between her legs. Her grip on his shaft tightened a little as she sucked in a breath, and Bryce felt her muscles tense up and release. He worked slow circles against her, finding her both familiar and completely different. Her body had changed a little since the last time he'd known her like this. He could feel the thin, hard line of a scar against his palm. Her hips were a little wider, a subtle change that a human might not notice, yet one that he both observed and appreciated. As she crushed herself against him and he felt the heaviness of her breasts against his chest, he knew that she wasn't the slim little waif she'd been. Dakota had bloomed into something even more magnificent than he'd known before.

She broke their kiss, clutching at his shoulder and pressing her forehead into his neck. Gasps escaped from her lips as he slipped one finger inside her and then out again, slick as he zeroed in on her center of pleasure. Bryce could feel her body coiling like a spring before she abandoned all control, crying out into the night. Her breath fluttered against his skin as she surrendered to her satisfaction.

Bryce lost the last remaining bit of control he had when she turned her head and grazed her teeth against his shoulder. Both sides of him went crazy with desire and the last few pieces of clothing quickly disappeared. He pulled her underneath him, his hands strong on her hips. Dakota's eyes were heavy with desire, and as she spread her thighs in invitation, Bryce plunged into her depths.

The world around them dissolved into inky blackness. Bryce no longer knew if he was a wolf, a man, or both as sheer ecstasy washed over his entire body. He moved his hips slowly, relishing the slide of his flesh against hers. His muscles clenched and his nerves sizzled. He wanted to live in this state and never let it be over, but he could feel his body fighting him. Bryce squeezed his eyelids together as their bodies moved in unison and he reached the ultimate height of contentment.

They lay there together for a while, stroking their fingers gently over each other's bodies. Bryce let himself enjoy the moment, but he knew they would be parting ways again very soon. It was the best for both of them, but it wouldn't be easy to convince his wolf.

6

"You've hardly touched your eggs."

Dakota blinked and looked up at her mother. Frankie had done her hair in a French braid and fastened the end with a silver barrette studded with crystals. It was one of the new baubles she'd found downtown when she and Kipp had gone shopping. Her mom always knew how to make the most out of a situation, whether she was living at home alone as a widow or hitting the road with her daughter in a tour bus.

"Sorry. I've just got a lot on my mind." Dakota picked up her fork, but she wasn't sure she could get the eggs down.

"At least eat the biscuit. It's not easy to make homemade biscuits without a full kitchen, even as nice as this bus is." Frankie gestured to Tyler, who was already filling his plate for the second time. "See, he knows how to appreciate good cooking."

Tyler grunted in agreement as he smeared one biscuit with jelly and another with butter and a drizzle of honey. He gave a rare grin as he sat down. "I like making the other guys at the agency jealous with this good food. There's a list of them ready to take my place if I ever quit."

"Don't you dare do something silly like that," Frankie threatened. "We've gotten used to you lurking around here, and I don't want to have to train a new bodyguard."

The two of them continued to kid around with each other as Dakota poked at her breakfast. She'd gone out in hopes of finding Bryce, but it was like fate had been on her side when she'd found him right outside the bus. She'd probably never have found him otherwise. Their little date at the carnival had been incredibly fun, and for the most part, she'd been able to forget all her concerns about her celebrity status. She'd even been close to telling Bryce her secret, but in the light of day, she was glad she hadn't. At the very least, it had been nice to forget about her stalker for a while. Dakota hadn't realized how much she'd still been on the lookout for him until Bryce had pointed out how much she was looking around. He had no idea just how awkward he'd made her feel when he'd asked her about Kipp's father.

"Tyler," she said once she'd forced herself to swallow a bite of eggs. "Do you think there's any chance I could've seen Rory Black last night?"

His fork clanked to his plate and he gave her a solemn look of disapproval. "I'd be able to answer that with more accuracy if you hadn't gone wandering off by yourself last night."

"I'm sorry for that." Well, she wasn't sorry for having done it. She *was* sorry for how much trouble and worry it caused him. He couldn't go against her wishes since she was his employer, but he couldn't do the job he was hired for if he wasn't around. "I just went out to the carnival for a little while. I wanted to see things the way I used to, and I did. But I think I might have seen him. At the very least, I saw a man who looked like him."

"Wouldn't he have recognized you and approached you if it was him?" Frankie suggested.

That was reasonable enough, but Dakota wasn't sure it made her feel any better.

Tyler wiped his mouth and reached into his pocket for his cell phone. "While I don't know exactly who you saw, I can tell you that someone I suspect to be Rory has been leaving comments all over your social media."

"You check that?" Dakota mostly left all that to her manager. It wasn't that she didn't want to interact with her fans, but she just didn't have the time to do it all personally.

"When it comes to your safety, I try to look at every aspect. I've already discussed it with Ray and told him to keep an eye on it, and the agency will be in contact with your upcoming venues so that their security teams can work with us on this. I've got it handled. I could handle it even better if you would cooperate with me." He gave her a pointed look before he picked up his fork again.

"Yeah." She wasn't going to go into that conversation any deeper. Tyler was right in many ways. If Dakota was worried about Rory Black, then she should be doing everything in her power to protect herself instead of making Tyler's life so difficult. On the other hand, she never would've had such a fabulous night with Bryce.

"I think I'm gonna go work on a couple of songs." She pushed her plate away and headed into the bedroom, but her fingers were limp against the strings of her guitar as soon as she picked it up. Her mind only wanted to focus on Bryce. He knew how to take charge, yet there was always that slight bit of hesitation that let her know he was concerned for what she truly wanted. Still, she knew there was a wild side to him. It was the sort of thing that would always force her to keep him at arm's length. He could only mean heartache and trouble, no matter how attractive he was.

She plucked a few strings as she thought about the way he'd made her entire body sizzle with delight, of how he'd made sure she was satisfied before he took his own pleasure. Those strong arms of his had been tantalizing under his shirt sleeves, but they'd been absolutely delicious when clothes didn't obstruct her view. Not to mention the way his abs rippled down to the treasure that awaited her below, one that she hadn't had nearly enough time to experience.

Dakota shook her head. Bryce had been one hell of a distraction. She hadn't allowed herself that sort of distraction for a long time. She was too busy working on her career and trying to raise Kipp without feeling like she'd left his care completely to Frankie. It was almost sad to think it would all be over in a few days, when the bus would have to head on to the next stop.

Her cell phone rang loudly, nearly making her drop her guitar. Dakota carefully laid it on the bed next to her and saw that it was Ray. Good. Maybe he'd actually listened to Tyler and she could get out of doing the Sheridan concert after all. Dakota wanted more time with Bryce, but she still wasn't sure she was comfortable staying there. "Hey, Ray."

"Hey? You're at the top of the charts and all you can say is 'hey?' You should be shouting from the rooftops!"

Dakota rolled her eyes. Yes, it was gratifying to see her songs rising through the ranks, but she'd hardly paid attention over the last few days. There was too much on her mind. "I've just been a little busy. What's up?"

"I just wanted to call you personally to firm up the rest of your tour. There have been a few small changes. The show in St. Louis has been pushed back by a couple of days to allow for an extra concert in Branson. The ticket pre-sales have already gone through the roof, and it only makes sense to take advantage of it. You can easily sell out a second night at the arena without the trouble of traveling. Anyway, once you're done in St. Louis, you'll be heading down to Nashville..."

Ray rattled on as Dakota twisted the phone away

from her face so he wouldn't hear her sigh. She'd been so excited when she first started this touring season, but now, she just felt like she was waiting for it to be over. No matter what city she went to next, she'd be worried about Rory Black. If she was honest with herself, she'd probably also be wishing that she could get away and have a little fun with Bryce. That would be impossible.

"So, that sums up all that, and I'll email you all the finalized dates," Ray said. "Now we need to talk about the *really* exciting part."

"Oh?" Probably an award nomination. Ray always went ballistic over those.

"The Sheridan Rodeo is having a charity auction to benefit a local children's home, and I told them you'd be more than happy to contribute."

Well, that was less work than attending an awards ceremony, although she wouldn't have minded an excuse to buy a new dress. "Sure. Some autographed albums and a t-shirt, or a meet-and-greet after the concert?"

Ray laughed. "No, it's not that type of auction. It's a bachelor and bachelorette auction. You—plus other local celebrities and some of the rodeo stars— will be up for grabs. The lucky winner will get to have dinner with you while you're there in Sheridan."

"You've got to be shitting me, Ray." Dakota lifted her eyes to the ceiling and wondered if she should get a new manager, despite how good he'd been for her career. "I can't do that. Tyler told you my stalker is here in town."

"Sure, babe, but he's on it. That's his job, and my job is to keep you in the spotlight. You've got the potential to be a long-term celebrity, someone who's a consistent hit for decades. It's not just talent, though. You have to keep working at it. Once you're a Reba McEntire or a Dolly Parton, it'll be smooth sailing."

"I don't want to do it, Ray." Dakota got to her feet and restlessly moved through the room, picking up a stray sock and straightening the beauty products on her dresser, doing anything that would make her feel more normal. It had taken quite some time to get used to bigger stages and massive crowds, and it had been surprisingly hard. Now she was going to be auctioned off like a piece of meat to God knew who.

"It's for a children's home, Dakota." Ray was getting that serious tone again. It was similar to the one she got from Tyler when she didn't listen to his advice, but at least with the bodyguard, Dakota knew he was truly looking out for her own good. Ray was just looking out for his pockets.

"Then I'll make a large monetary donation," Dakota reasoned. "Actually, I'll even donate my time. I'll spend an afternoon down at the children's home myself, handing out books and blankets and whatever else they might want. That sounds a heck of a lot better than this auction."

"Have I steered you wrong yet?" Ray challenged. "When you said you weren't good enough to go on the road and that no one would show up at your concerts, who was the one who promised you they'd come? And they did. What about when you were concerned that the music you wrote yourself wouldn't be nearly as good as what the pro writers sold to us, and you thought your next album was going to tank? But I knew better, and I pushed you to put yourself out there. It was your heart and soul and all that you put into the music that made you so good, and the fans adored it. They still do, and if they think there's even a minute chance they could win a dinner with you, they're going to believe in you that much more. The people who can't afford to win you in an auction will fill the void in their hearts by streaming all your music, buying your albums, and piddling away their paychecks on your merch. I haven't been wrong yet, Dakota, and I'm not wrong now."

Damn. That was hard to argue with. People had always said she had a good voice, and she knew how much of herself she put into her music, but no one would ever have heard her if Ray hadn't pushed her the way he had. "Fine. But I don't have to like it."

"Nope. You just have to pretend to. Plaster a smile on your face, play nice, and of course, Tyler will be there with you. It'll all be fine. Trust me."

When she got off the phone, Dakota didn't bother picking her guitar back up. She didn't feel like writing a new song anymore. She loved what she did for a living. Her career was fabulous, and she was so lucky to get to share her art with the world. But she'd be willing to bet that no one understood just how hard it was.

7

"CAN I GO AGAIN?" THE LITTLE GIRL ASKED, GRINNING over her shoulder at Bryce.

"You have to go to the back of the line so everyone has a turn," he explained for the millionth time as he helped her down off the old pony.

"Aw." She frowned deeply, but she paused to kiss the pony's muzzle. "Can I have this one again when it's my turn?"

"I'll see what I can do." The sun was beating down, and the minimal breeze wasn't doing much to dissipate the heat. Bryce was more than used to being out in the elements, so he wouldn't have minded in the least if he were out herding cattle or repairing a fence. But it was his day to be stuck running the pony rides. Actually, it was supposed to be Zane's turn, but he'd made another excuse about his sick aunt and had hardly been around at all.

With a sigh, Bryce opened the gate to let in the next four children. He didn't mind kids. It wasn't really the weather. What truly bothered him was that working there meant he was within a stone's throw of Dakota's bus, yet he couldn't be near her. Not that he'd have any guarantee of being able to see her anyway. She'd mentioned something about a bodyguard, and Bryce knew his looks would get him turned away in an instant, no matter what his intentions were. He briefly wondered if Dakota had any control over that, but then he shoved the thought aside. He'd meant to bring her back to her door once they'd gotten dressed and he'd driven his truck back into town, but Dakota had insisted on being dropped off in the parking lot. That told him all that he needed to know. She could claim she wasn't embarrassed to be with him or that she wasn't involved with anyone else, but she obviously wanted to keep him a secret.

He wasn't sure that he minded, but his wolf had been a restless mess ever since he'd left her there. It couldn't understand that there was much more to this whole situation than just doing what it wanted. If he caved and gave into that beast, he'd be at her side constantly throughout the day and waiting in the wings during her concerts. If she wouldn't allow him near her, then he'd be lurking nearby and waiting for his chance to convince her otherwise. *Like that would go over well,* he chided himself. *The last thing she needs is a stalker.*

"I'm scared!" The little voice cut through his reverie, and Bryce saw the boy who'd hesitated just inside the gate as he stared up at the ponies.

It was hard for Bryce to understand anyone being afraid of a horse, especially the old ones that were usually used for pony rides. Still, there was something about the fear in the kid's voice that plucked at his heart the moment he heard it. As he approached him to explain just how safe this whole thing was, Bryce realized he'd seen this kid before.

"It's all right, Kipp." An older woman was hovering nearby, and she smiled gently at the boy as she waved toward the ponies. "They're very nice horsies, or else they wouldn't let them be here. They have to behave themselves."

Bryce had only caught a glimpse of Dakota's son outside the bus and from a distance, but with a name like that, he had zero doubt that this was the same boy. He looked just like her, with those dark, almond-shaped eyes and a touch of red to his hair.

His chubby cheeks were still smooth with youth, but Bryce wouldn't have been surprised if in a few years, that baby fat melted away to reveal some major cheekbones.

He lifted his glance to the woman. Grandmother? Maybe. Dakota could probably afford to hire the highest-end nanny on the planet, but he'd been willing to gamble she was a relative at the very least. Her hair was darker and the shape of her face was different, but the eyes were similar.

His mouth dried up like the desert as he checked the area. Dakota was nowhere around. He already knew that because he would've felt her if she was there, but he'd hoped to find her anyway. Instead, he crouched down in front of the little boy. "She's right, you know. These are the nicest horses you'll find in all of Wyoming."

"Really?" His eyes widened, a look he'd seen on Dakota's face before.

"Sure." The wind changed just then, and Bryce caught a scent that nearly sent him reeling backward. It was faint, but he could swear the kid was a shifter. There was something familiar about that scent, too, something he couldn't quite wrap his head around. He swallowed as he held his hand out. "Come here. You can meet Scout."

"Scout?" Kipp hesitated a little as they approached the pony.

"Yep. Why don't you pet him?" Bryce felt as though everyone on the fairgrounds was staring at him, even though probably not a soul was paying attention to him other than Kipp and his grand-mother. He had to be wrong. He knew without even a smidgen of doubt that Dakota was a human. She didn't have a drop of shifter blood in her. But that meant Kipp's father...

"He's nice!" Kipp giggled. The fear had left his eyes completely and was replaced by pure joy as the old pony's whiskers grazed against his knuckles. "Can I ride him?"

"Sure thing. That's what you're here for. Come on." He lifted Kipp and settled him into the saddle.

His stomach flipped. Bryce wanted to be wrong, but his senses hadn't failed him before. He relied on them as a shifter because he knew he had one hell of a secret to keep. He could tell the difference between a human and a shifter, and there was definitely an animal inside this boy. It was faint, and as Bryce moved off to help the other children, he decided Kipp had probably not experienced his other side yet.

It was enough of a shock to find out that Kipp

was a shifter, but Bryce had been slammed with information far more earth-shattering. He tried to chase it away with logic as he clucked to the ponies to get started, but it was impossible. The timing was right. Kipp was his son. He leaned against the fence and tried to figure out how he was ever going to wrap his head around it.

"Thanks for that." The grandmother stepped up behind him, leaning on the outside of the little corral. "Kipp has been really excited about coming here, and he's obsessed with cowboys these days. I'd hate for this experience to have turned him off."

"Not a problem." Bryce felt a sheen of sweat forming on his forehead. If this woman *was* Dakota's mother, did she have any idea? Would she tell him anything if he asked? Hell, Bryce wasn't even sure what he should ask. His mind was reeling. This was all so impossible.

He watched Kipp closely, studying his little hands as they wrapped around the saddle horn. The boy tipped his head back slightly as he grinned. "He seems to be enjoying himself."

"That's something Kipp doesn't have a problem doing," the older woman replied with a smile. "I was actually pretty surprised at his hesitation when it came to the pony ride. He usually throws himself into anything that looks fun."

Bryce tried not to think that Kipp could've inherited that trait from him. Sure, he had a steady job, but he'd done some crazy stuff in his life and damned the consequences. "The ponies are small to us, but I guess they probably look pretty big to kids."

It wasn't long before the ride was over, and Bryce stepped forward to bring the ponies to a halt. He helped all the other children to the ground before he went around to Scout and offered a hand to Kipp. "Have fun?"

"Yeah! Thank you!" Kipp threw his arms around Bryce.

It was the strangest feeling. Even his wolf was a little confused as he lifted the boy down. He didn't know this child. He had no reason to feel anything fatherly toward him, yet he knew in that moment that should some danger descend upon him, he would throw himself in harm's way to save Kipp's life. Sweat now dripped down his temples. "You're welcome," he choked out.

Kipp and his grandmother waved goodbye as they moved off toward the petting zoo. Bryce watched them go for a moment before he forced himself to return to the task at hand, and he was glad that this was a pretty mindless job. A series of emotions moved through him one after the other, each one drowning him and giving him no chance to work through it before the next one took over. He felt panic at the idea that he had created a life in this world, and guilt over not having done anything to contribute. Anger boiled his blood as he realized that Dakota had never bothered to tell him, and she'd certainly had a chance last night. Fear of the future came next. Was this why Dakota was in town? Had she arranged to have a concert there so she could make him step up and be a father figure? Bryce already knew he didn't qualify to be a good mate, so how could he possibly raise a child?

Finally, Caleb showed up to take over for the evening shift. He lifted a brow over his friendly blue eyes. "Were the kids that hard on you? You look dead on your feet."

"Yeah. You could say that. I'll see ya." Bryce didn't bother sticking around for small talk and headed for his truck. He paused at the edge of the parking lot and considered turning around. It would only be a short walk over to Dakota's tour bus. He could insist he talk to her, no matter what any security personnel had to say about it, and ask her just why in the hell she hadn't told him.

No. He needed more time to think about this. He needed to be prepared before he talked to her, and that meant he'd need a little more time to go over this in his head and make sure he wasn't jumping to conclusions. Bryce had already been caught off-guard by this revelation, and he'd be damned if she was going to have the upper hand when he went to talk to her.

He drove too fast back to the Ward Ranch and headed straight for the bunkhouse. Unfortunately, being indoors in the air conditioning didn't do anything to ease his mind. It just made him feel like a caged animal, and the actual animal inside him was just as uneasy. There were so many questions, and he had no way of knowing the answers unless he spoke to Dakota. He was too angry to do that right now.

Regardless, he knew he had to act in some way. Bryce yanked his phone out of his pocket and quickly searched her name. Dakota Jones was all over the internet, just like any other celebrity these days. She had an official website, but Bryce skipped over that. He knew it wouldn't have any information she hadn't approved of. He skimmed through a Wikipedia page, but it focused on her discography more than anything else.

Articles from tabloids and entertainment magazines were lined up in the search results after that, and Bryce quickly lost himself in them. He studied photos of Kipp, looking for traces of himself in the boy's face. He held his breath when he found a photo of Dakota with a man, but it turned out to just be her bodyguard.

Bryce barely heard the door open when Zane came in. He glanced at his roommate. "Hey."

"Hey."

"How's your aunt doing?" Bryce was looking at his phone again. He'd found a photo of Dakota at some sort of awards ceremony. Normally, he didn't pay attention to that sort of thing at all, and he'd never even watched the Oscars on TV. In the picture, Dakota had paused on the red carpet for the photo op. Her hair had been caught in a loose bun at the nape of her neck, with tendrils of hair spiraling down on either side of her face. She'd donned a dress of pale gold that clung to her curves before it descended into a loose, romantic skirt that dragged out behind her. Bryce felt his heartbeat speed up.

"About the same," Zane grunted as he headed toward his room.

"Hey, are you going to the Dakota Jones concert?" Looking at this photo just threw her celebrity status in his face once again. In a few days, people would be piling into the grandstands at the fairgrounds to see her perform, hoping to get as close to her as possible.

Zane paused. He turned and gave Bryce a quizzical look. "Who?"

"Dakota Jones," he repeated impatiently. "The country singer. She's performing at the rodeo this week."

The ranch hand shrugged. "I guess not. I don't really keep up with that sort of thing."

"Sorry." Bryce put the phone down and swiped a hand over his face, realizing how obsessed he'd become with Dakota and now her son. *His* son. "I'm sure you're too occupied with your aunt to be concerned about a concert."

"Yeah. Pretty much." Zane didn't offer any other details before he disappeared into his room, but that was just how he was.

Bryce didn't bother trying to get involved in his personal life, and he had enough going on that he didn't need anyone else's problems. He was going to have to make some tough decisions.

8

DAKOTA STRUMMED A CHORD, BUT SHE'D FRETTED IT wrong and it sounded horrible. She cursed under her breath and tried again. She got it right this time, at least as far as her fingering was concerned, but it still wasn't the right chord for the song. Dakota picked up her pencil and scratched out the note.

She'd been trying to work on some new songs the entire time she'd been on the road. This was supposed to be the perfect time for her to compose, so that once she finally made it back into the studio, she'd have a ton of fresh material for the producer to manipulate. It never bothered her when someone suggested a change of notes or lyrics or the addition of a few extra instruments. Dakota felt that it usually added a lot to what she'd already put together, and the results had been hits so far. But she had to come up with the beginnings of those songs first.

This one was proving to be a challenge. It was supposed to be a typical road song about how hard it was to be on tour when you knew someone was waiting for you back home. It was the sort of thing that people would love. They would relate to it as they went off to college or on a business trip, and they would hug their loved ones even tighter when they returned. But so far, she'd barely gotten the opening melody plucked out on her guitar.

Frustrated, Dakota decided this one might be easier to tackle if she started with the words first. "It's hard out here with nothing but the road under my feet, and I look for you every time we turn onto a new street. Ugh. No." She flicked through the little journal she used to jot down words and phrases that came to her, and sometimes those turned into entire songs. Right now, it all sounded like total shit. She chucked it against the doorway.

"Problems?" Tyler called out from down the hall.

"None you can help me with." Dakota launched herself off the bed and came out into the living area to find him sitting in a recliner and scrolling through the news on his phone. The device was comically tiny in his hands. "Unless songwriting is a hidden talent you didn't tell me about."

Tyler raised one dark brow. "I think we'd both be better off if I stuck to security."

"Yeah, I figured." Dakota opened a cabinet and poked around until she found the coffee pods. She slammed one into the Keurig and clunked the top down. "I think I need a break. Being on the road is supposed to be romantic and inspiring, but I just feel exhausted and drained."

"Do you need a doctor?" Tyler put down his phone and watched her carefully. "I'm sure we can find one."

"No, it's not like that." Dakota found the hazelnut coffee creamer in the fridge and poured a generous serving in her mug. "I just need a vacation. And don't even tell me that I'm already on vacation because I'm traveling around the country."

He put his hands up in the air defensively. "Wasn't going to say a thing."

"It used to be that I'd get out into the woods when I wanted to get creative. I'd go for a hike or hang out by a lake. There's something about it that just makes you forget all about bills and taxes and contracts and what everyone else is expecting of you, and it's easier for me to let loose and write a song."

She'd written enough of them that it seemed like it should be easier by now, no matter what her circumstances were, but that just wasn't the case. At least not at the moment. Frustration was blocking her in, and she could almost feel it, thick and angry in her head.

"So let's go out for a hike," Tyler suggested. "I wouldn't mind getting off the bus for a little while, and I think there are quite a few places to hike near Sheridan." He picked up his phone again.

Dakota waved at him to put the phone down as she took a sip of hot coffee. "Don't bother. It's too late to try to do something like that today, and even if we did, it just wouldn't be the same knowing that I always had you looming over me. No offense."

"None taken." Tyler tapped his thick fingers on the arm of the recliner. "Is there something else you could do to improve your creativity?"

"Beats me." Dakota turned around and leaned against the kitchen counter. It didn't help that Bryce was still on her mind. Every time she thought about writing something passionate and lovey-dovey, his face swam up in her mind's eye. He was good-looking. He was fun to be with, and he made her forget the parts of her life that were hardest to deal with. But he was also exactly what she didn't need in her life. She'd leave him behind in Sheridan, and then she'd have to stop thinking about him. Right now, though, knowing he was never all that far away, it wasn't easy.

"Is it the stalker thing?" Tyler asked. "Because I know how upset you'd gotten about that before."

Dakota turned her head and looked out the window, not wanting to look Tyler in the eye. He wasn't wrong. She'd been extremely upset to know that someone was constantly trying to get as close to her as possible, and she'd had a bit of a breakdown over it shortly after Tyler had come onboard. "That was a lot earlier in my career," she reasoned. "I wasn't used to having fans at all, much less super-fans. I'm not really worried about that right now. I mean, it affects me in that he's the primary reason that I can't go out, but I'm sure someone else would be tracking me down even if he wasn't."

"Are you sure? It can't be easy on you, and the stress might really be building up."

She frowned into her coffee, unsure of what to say. Tyler was trying to help, she knew. He just didn't understand how hard this was. "I don't know. I'll figure it out. Maybe I just need to get the hell out of Sheridan. That, at least, will make me feel a little better."

The bus door opened. Kipp's footfalls preceded him as he clomped up the stairs and bounded into the living area. "Mommy! Guess what, guess what, guess what?"

"What, what, what?" she replied, glad that at least this distraction was worth it. Rory Black just made her life hard. Bryce made her uncertain. But Kipp? He was her everything. "Did you have a good day with Grandma?"

"I rode a horse! A really big horse!" He gestured wildly with his little hands.

"You did?" Dakota looked up at her mother, who was standing just behind Kipp.

Frankie shook her head and held her hand out hip-high, suggesting it'd just been a pony.

"Yes!" Kipp continued. "And his name was Scout! And he let me pet him. And he had a fat belly."

Dakota put one hand over her mouth so that Kipp wouldn't see her giggle. He was so damn cute when he got excited, and she didn't want him to ever be discouraged from that.

Meanwhile, Kipp was rambling on and on about his experience. "They had other horses there, too, but I got to ride the best one. And there was a little girl that cried, but not me. And your friend helped me get in the saddle."

That last part caught her ear more than the rest. "My friend?" Dakota didn't know anyone there.

"Yeah. The one with the drawings on his arms."

Shit. Dakota's stomach dropped all the way down into her feet and maybe out of the bottom of the bus. She tried to swallow, but her throat was too tight. "Oh, I see," she finally choked out, her voice too high and thin. "I didn't realize you knew my friend."

"I saw him out the window when you were talking to him."

"Right. Of course." Dakota kept her gaze firmly on Kipp, but she could feel both Tyler and Frankie looking at her. "What else did you do today?"

Her son chattered on about a petting zoo, but Dakota was hardly paying any attention now. She tried to tell herself it was no big deal that Kipp had seen Bryce. The boy hadn't necessarily seen him when she'd left the other night and run off with him. She'd talked to him on that very first day they'd arrived in Sheridan, and there hadn't been anything even slightly romantic about that encounter. She was going to have to be more careful, though. Dakota had decided a long time ago that she was going to keep Bryce out of their son's life, and it was a decision that would be best for all of them.

"And then when I got to pet the llama, it took the

whole cup of food and dumped it on the ground,"
Kipp explained. "Grandma bought me another one."

"I'm sure she did. I think you'd better go get
ready for your bath, little man. You smell like you
belong at the petting zoo." Dakota tickled his belly.

"No, I don't!" Kipp giggled, making only the
weakest effort at fending off the tickles. "I'm a wolf,
and they don't have wolves at the petting zoo!"
Finally, he ran off to get his pajamas.

"The wolf thing again, huh? After his tale about
riding that horse, I thought he'd be entering in the
rodeo himself," she commented when he'd shut the
door to his little room.

"Trust me, he was very proud of himself. I
thought he might ask me for a pair of spurs." Frankie
moved to the kitchen sink to wash her hands. "You
didn't tell me you knew the guy running the pony
rides."

"Only sort of, and I didn't know he'd be running
the pony rides." Dakota's insides were still shaking,
even though she'd tried to find enough logic in the
situation to make herself feel better. "He's just
someone who remembers me from the last time I
played here."

"I see." Her mother dried her hands off and got a
bottle of water from the fridge.

Dakota could tell she wanted to ask more questions, and there was a chance they would come later, but Frankie was at least holding off for now. Even her mother didn't know who had fathered Kipp, and Dakota preferred to keep that secret to herself.

"Any chance he's got anything to do with Rory Black?" Tyler asked.

"What? No. He..." She trailed off for a split second, trying to come up with some good excuse for knowing Bryce. "He was helping to set up the stage when I'd played here before. That's all." It was a big, fat lie, but if it would get her through the moment without furthering the inquisition, then she was willing to go with it.

"Can I use the bubble bath?" Kipp shouted as he came out of his room and headed for the bathroom.

"Hang on. I'm coming." Dakota moved off down the hall after him.

"I can do that," Frankie offered.

"I know, but I want to." Dakota had music to write, and she knew her mother had been genuine in her offer. But she wanted to spend as much time with Kipp as possible, and it wasn't like she was going to get a single note written with this whole thing about Bryce hanging over her head. She joined Kipp in the bathroom, running the water and putting plenty of bubble bath into the tub. "So it sounds like you had a pretty good day."

Kipp plunked himself down into the tub and giggled as he swished the bubbles around with his hands. "Yep!"

Dakota twisted her lips, trying to decide if she wanted to ask Kipp anything further about Bryce. She was dying to know every single detail of their interaction. As far as Kipp was concerned, it had obviously gone well since he seemed thrilled with his pony ride. But what about Bryce? Was there any chance that he'd figured out that Kipp was actually his?

She grabbed a washcloth out of the linen closet and handed it to Kipp, studying his sweet little face. It was hard not to imagine just how difficult of a conversation that would be. Bryce would be angry, and he'd have every right to be. Dakota hadn't told him, and she hadn't even made any effort to find him when she'd discovered she was pregnant. But Bryce just wasn't the sort of guy to play house with. He was a bad boy, the love-'em-and-leave-'em type. She'd known it as soon as she'd met him five years ago, and she'd been fine with it since she didn't have any intention of sticking around and turning into a homemaker.

But what was Bryce playing at, spending time with Kipp?

No. She didn't need to think that way. Dakota was getting in her head too much. Kipp meeting his biological father had been a pure accident, and Kipp was the spitting image of Dakota. "Here, honey. Let's get your hair washed."

9

It had only been a few hours since Bryce had left the fairgrounds before he found himself pulling into the parking lot once again. There were even more people than there'd been before, and he had to wind through multiple rows of vehicles before he finally found a free spot. It wasn't helping his nerves at all.

He sucked in a deep breath as he got out and began walking. This might be a huge mistake. Coming back and talking to Dakota might urge her to cut him out of her life and ruin even the slimmest chance for the two of them to be together. But then, that was how life was going to go anyway, right? They were completely incompatible, and no matter how hard they tried, it just wasn't going to work.

Bryce reasoned that he wasn't ruining his chances with Dakota when they were already doomed.

The sun had nearly disappeared behind the horizon. The shadows were deep under the trees and between the various campers and horse trailers, and they were made even deeper as the lights began to turn on. Bryce wished real life could be more like that, where it was more obvious what was right and what was wrong. Instead, he was just stumbling along through a gray area.

A large man was standing outside the bus, leaning against the side. He tilted his head back to peer into the night sky, but then he scanned the area. His eyes met Bryce's.

This was the same bodyguard Bryce had seen in some of the photographs of Dakota online. Tyler, Bryce thought his name was. There'd been some article that had mentioned how Dakota had kept the same bodyguard over the last few years. He was massive, but what Bryce found far more interesting was that he was a shifter. He could tell right away. Was there any chance that this guy was Kipp's father instead? No. It would explain the animal inside Kipp, but not the way he smelled.

"Can I do something for you?" Tyler watched Bryce carefully.

"I'm here to see Dakota." Bryce stepped forward into the bit of light near the bus.

"Oh. I thought you might be someone else." The hand that had reached toward a hidden weapon relaxed a bit.

"Someone dangerous enough to need a gun?" Bryce asked. He hadn't expected anyone to roll out the welcome mat for him, but the reaction seemed a little extreme.

Tyler's eyes roved down Bryce's arms, taking in the tattoos. "You're the one she took off with the other night."

"I guess you could say that." Bryce didn't think anyone had seen him, but apparently, he was wrong. Of course, if Dakota's bodyguard was a shifter, then he was probably damn good at his job.

"Good. Then you're not the one I'm looking for."

"What the hell are you talking about? I'm just here to see Dakota." Bryce was losing patience. This goon would let him see Dakota or not, but he didn't want to stand out there and get dicked around.

The bus door swung open. "Tyler, I—oh. Hi, Bryce." Dakota was dressed in a tank top and a pair of terrycloth shorts that accentuated the curves of her bare legs.

Irritation rushed over Bryce's skin as he noticed

Tyler take a couple of steps closer to Dakota. There was no reason for the guard to protect her from him. He moved closer as well. "I want to talk to you. No. I *need* to talk to you." He'd already gotten himself as psyched up for this moment as he could, and he didn't want to give it up now.

Dakota moved down a step, but Tyler blocked the doorway. "It's late, and things have only been getting worse," he growled.

She blew a breath out between her lips as she scanned the area around them. "I'll be all right. I won't be long. I promise."

Tyler's body was tense as he stepped back, forced into obedience by his boss. "Fine. But I'll be right here."

Tyler wasn't the only one who was tense. Bryce could sense the anxiety in Dakota as she came down off the last step and charged through the grass toward him. She passed him, making Bryce quickly turn to follow her.

"What was all that about?" he demanded.

"What was what about?" Dakota stopped under a tree. Light and shadow filtered down through the leaves and dappled her face.

"Your bodyguard was just about to pull a gun on me. He said he thought I was someone else. Who the hell is he worried about?" *And why is he a shifter? Is my son in danger?* Those questions would have to wait. One at a time.

Dakota flapped a hand through the air. "It's just this stalker that's been following me around for a while. It's nothing."

"Nothing?" It sure didn't feel like nothing to him. Anger boiled in his blood and made a heady mixture with his urge to protect her. It already felt wrong to Bryce that she should have some other shifter looking after her, no matter that it was simply a paid position. "Who is this guy?"

"I don't know, and I really don't want to talk about it. I'm tired and I'm cranky, and I didn't expect to see you here tonight. What's going on?" She crossed her arms in front of her chest.

The thin material clung to her, revealing the roundness of her breasts and the shape of her nipples. Bryce forced his eyes back to her face. He took a second to pull himself back together once again. What was it about Dakota that always made him fall apart? "I already know, but I want to hear it from you. Is Kipp my son?"

Dakota's face changed instantly. Her brows had been drawn down in irritation, making a congruent line with the hardness of her mouth. But now her face went entirely blank as her head bobbed back slightly on her neck, making her look as though something had hit her and left her stunned. She licked her lips. "What gives you that idea?"

He could leave it at that. Her lack of a real answer was an answer in itself, but he wasn't going to just let her roll out of Sheridan on nothing more than speculation. "Dakota, I can tell. There are too many things that line up. I want the truth, damn it. I deserve it." He curled his fingers into a fist and resisted the urge to pound it against the tree trunk out of sheer exasperation.

She swallowed and looked down at the ground. When Dakota looked up again, her face was neutral and stony. "Fine. Kipp is your son."

Bryce closed his eyes for a moment as his head reeled. His wolf was going nuts inside him. He had a son. He had a child that he'd helped bring into the world. There was so much he needed to teach him, to share with him. Both fear and joy rushed through his body. How could he ever be a father? How could he do this?

"But don't worry," Dakota said, interrupting his thoughts. "Kipp and I have been doing just fine on our own, and I don't want anything from you."

"Now, hold on a second. If I was worried about

that, I don't think I would've shown up here and asked you. You've been doing a damn good job of keeping this little secret from me for the last five years, and I could have just as easily let it go and pretended that he was your love child with that hired gun."

The implication set her ablaze. Even in the dim light, Dakota had a fire in her dark eyes as she reached out and shoved her open hands at Bryce's chest. "How dare you even say such a thing?"

"Because he—never mind." There was only one reason that Bryce had even considered the idea, and it was because Tyler was a shifter. Not the same species as him, but a shifter all the same. Explaining that would mean calling himself out on what he truly was, and Dakota didn't know. Did she? "I'm just pissed off, okay?"

"Fine. Then be pissed off. I don't really care. But that doesn't mean you can go around saying stuff like that. My life is nothing but rumors, and I've worked really hard to keep the worst ones at bay. Someone is constantly watching me, whether it means I'm under Tyler's thumb or someone is pointing a camera at me. Every single thing I do and every word I say has the potential to create headlines. Do you understand?" Dakota was practically shouting now, and tears glistened in her eyes.

"Yeah. I think I do. You wouldn't want the whole world to know that your child was fathered by some lowlife you shacked up with for a couple of days while you were on the road. You wouldn't want anyone to think that the sweet Dakota Jones had lowered herself enough to be with a guy like me. Yeah, I understand just fine." He took a step back. All of this was going horribly wrong. He hadn't wanted to try to step in and play house, so he should've been thrilled that Dakota wanted to keep the status quo. His wolf snarled in rage and confusion, wanting to be angry but not angry at Dakota because she was his mate. Bryce leaned against the tree, almost dizzy with all these conflicting emotions.

"It's just not as simple as it probably seems from the outside," Dakota said quietly. "I've been doing what I thought was best."

"Yeah." It was all he could muster for the moment. Bryce was going to need time to think about this. He had to know about Kipp, but he couldn't just come right out and tell Dakota the truth about himself. Could he? Hell, what would happen if Kipp shifted and someone happened to catch it on camera? He didn't know how he was going to deal with this. "At least, just tell me, is Kipp all right? Does he have any health issues or anything I should know about?"

"Ten fingers and ten toes," Dakota quipped. "And a healthy dose of wild boy energy."

"Okay." He pressed his hand to his head, still toying with the idea of telling her. She was going to need to know. If Kipp hadn't shifted yet, then he would eventually. Of course, it wasn't as though she would believe him, even if he did tell her the truth. He pushed himself off the tree, forcing his feet to carry him once again. "I'll, um, I'll leave you be, then."

Dakota began moving back toward the bus, but she hesitated. "Bryce, I'm sorry."

"Me, too." He stayed in place long enough to make sure Dakota got back under the watchful eye of Tyler, but then he stumbled back to his truck. He sat behind the wheel for a long time, not even seeing all the cars and activity that surrounded him. There were people all around him, screaming with laughter as they headed to the rodeo and all the events that went along with it. They had no idea that his world had been brought to a crashing halt, and everything went on whether he was a part of it or not. That was exactly how this whole thing with Kipp felt. There were things happening that he was supposed to be a part of, yet he'd been left behind.

Bryce had thought he'd be better off knowing for certain, not having to question and wonder for the rest of his life. Now he wasn't so sure. He pounded the steering wheel and started the ignition.

10

"KEEP THOSE PADDLES GOING, LADIES, BECAUSE THIS IS a once-in-a-lifetime chance! We've got our very own rodeo star Ace McCarthy on the auction block!"

The audience went wild with female screams as the young man stepped out next to the auctioneer. He waved shyly, but Dakota caught the glimmer of excitement in his eyes.

"The lucky lady who wins this auction will not only get to head out on the town for a delicious dinner with Ace, but a private trail ride as well! So saddle up, ladies. It's time to flash some cash for the children's home! Do I hear fifty? Of course, I do. How about seventy-five? There it is!"

Dakota smiled to herself as she watched the embarrassed cowboy bring in bid after bid. It had been easy to get caught up in the event and forget about her stalker or the songs she couldn't quite get written. She'd certainly been glad to forget about that discussion with Bryce the night before. Dakota still hadn't been able to figure out how he knew. Nobody knew, not even Kipp or Frankie. He was in on the secret now, and she couldn't take it back.

"One-fifty!"

Ace McCarthy's cheeks were getting pinker by the second.

"Careful, now," Tyler said. He stood next to her, lurking in the wings and watching the crowd. "If you keep smiling like that, someone might think you're actually enjoying yourself."

"Maybe I am," she retorted. "Just don't tell Ray. I don't want him to think I'm willing to do this sort of thing on the regular. In fact, if he asks me again, I'm telling him no. Flat out."

"Sure. And yet you're standing here grinning like an idiot," he said pointedly.

Hearing him talk so bluntly only made Dakota smile a little more. She liked how honest her bodyguard allowed himself to be. "Look at the crowd. They're going nuts. I guess it's just amusing to see it happen to someone else. I won't enjoy it nearly as much when it's my turn."

"Two-fifty!" the auctioneer boomed. "Can we crank it up to three hundred? Thank you, ma'am! Three-fifty?"

"It'll certainly be amusing to see who gets a hold of that guy. That woman bidding on him in the front row looks like she's going to eat him alive if she manages to get him." Tyler nodded toward the woman, who was waving her paddle and screaming.

"She'll wear him out before he ever gets a chance to compete in his event," Dakota laughed. "I guess at least he knows he's appreciated around here. I can only hope I do as well."

"Five hundred!" the auctioneer shouted. "Can we keep it going?"

"Are you kidding? The only reason anyone has held back on the other auctions so far is because they're saving up for you. I'm sure they're excited for a news anchor or a radio personality, but that's not nearly as exciting as an actual country star. Of course, Ray didn't bother asking me how I was going to deal with security on this one. I guess that means the winner will be getting a date with me as well." Tyler waggled his eyebrows.

He was in a good mood, and Dakota couldn't blame him. There was so much excitement coming from the grandstands, and it gave her hope that this wouldn't turn out to be nearly as awful as she'd imagined when Ray had first told her about it.

"Excuse me." A woman approached, moving slowly as though Dakota might go running off if she got spooked. Her eyes roved over Tyler's hulking frame. "Um, I'm so sorry to bother you. It's just that I'm here for the auction, as well, and I'm a huge fan. I was wondering if I might be able to get a picture with you."

Tyler looked uncomfortable, but Dakota quickly smiled and nodded. "Of course. What's your name?"

"Shari. Shari Oakley," she beamed. "I'm the high school principal, so I've gotten roped into this thing. Some of my students are living in the children's home, and it means an awful lot to me that so many people—especially you—have come out to help us."

Something touched Dakota's heart, and she realized how selfish she'd been to not want to do this charity auction originally. "Is the home that bad off?"

"Well, we've lost a lot of our funding," Shari admitted. Her large eyes drooped down slightly at the outer corners, giving her that sad hound dog look. "We've had some private donors that have had to drop out due to financial issues, and it's just really hard to get anyone to look twice at these kids who've come from abusive homes or have parents in jail. A decent amount of them have behavioral or mental health problems, which makes it that much harder."

"I'm so sorry," Dakota said genuinely. She couldn't even imagine what it would be like to live without Kipp. She planned to give him a huge hug as soon as she got back to the tour bus. "I'd love to help out. If you can give me the address, I'll have a check sent over."

"Really? Oh, please don't think I came over here to ask for money!" Shari looked both thrilled and embarrassed.

That wasn't an uncommon reaction when Dakota met people while out on tour, though. "I know you weren't. I just want to do what I can to help. Hopefully, I'll pull a little money in here at the auction, but I'd like to do more where I can."

"You're a saint!" Shari handed over her business card on which she'd written the name and address of the children's home on the back.

Dakota instructed Tyler to help, and he obliged as the two women took a series of both serious and goofy shots together. They were laughing so hard they were practically in tears by the end of it. Dakota couldn't explain why, but she just instantly clicked with Shari. When she finally pulled her arm out from around her shoulders, she wished for a moment that she was just another local and she could invite Shari out to lunch. There was a sense of normalcy in that idea that gave her a pang of wistfulness.

Tyler handed Shari her phone and nodded at Dakota. "Looks like you're on."

"Ladies and gentlemen, it's the moment you've all been waiting for," the auctioneer announced. The grandstands thundered with cheers.

"Thank you again. And good luck!" Shari said before she moved off into the wings of the stage that had been set up for the event.

"Oh, boy." Dakota's stomach contracted as she combed her fingers through her hair and straightened the skirt of her dress. "How's my makeup?"

"It's fine, but you could look like a clown and they'd still eat you up," Tyler pointed out.

"Not very helpful," Dakota said with a smile. "I'm nervous."

"No need to be. All you have to do is stand there. No singing or playing the guitar today. They just love you for who you are."

She smiled up at him, but she kept herself from making any remarks about how sweet he was. Dakota knew he hated that, even though that was one of the many reasons she kept him on. Tyler kept her safe physically, but he was great at giving her emotional support when she needed it, too. "Okay. I'm ready."

"You've heard her on the radio. You've seen her on TV. Most of you probably have tickets for her concert that will be taking place right here on this stage. Let's give a big Sheridan welcome to none other than Dakota Jones!"

Dakota stepped out of the wings and onto the stage. She threw her arms out to wave and blow kisses at the audience. She always felt like a different person when she was onstage. Her nerves and doubts always ended up getting left behind with that first step, no matter how shaky she'd been only a moment before. She couldn't stop smiling as she took in the vast crowd that had assembled for the auction.

"Miss Jones, I can't tell you how delighted we are to have you here. Is there anything you'd like to say?" The auctioneer pressed the mic at her.

"Oh." She hadn't been prepared for that, but she took the mic and went for it. "I want to thank you all so much for making me feel welcome here. I'd also like to remind you of just how important it is that we support organizations like the children's home that are doing so much for the local youth. It's hard work, and so much of it takes place behind the scenes where no one notices. I've already pledged to make a private donation regardless of how high this auction goes tonight, and I urge you all to do the same. Even just a few dollars can make a difference." She handed the mic back as the crowd once again exploded with applause.

"All right, folks. There you have it, straight from the top country star's mouth. Miss Jones has pledged a dinner as well as some signed merchandise and VIP tickets for the concert. Shall we get the bidding started? Do I hear five hundred?"

Dakota raised her eyebrows, surprised that the opening bid was ten times higher than what it had been for the others. But someone immediately flashed their number and the bids quickly increased. Dakota studied the audience. She focused on one person after another, seeing all those eager faces and wondering what their lives were like. Would they go to work on Monday and talk about what a ridiculous price someone was willing to pay for a dinner date with her? Or would they be disappointed that they weren't the winners? Either way, their lives stood to be far more normal than hers would ever be.

She lifted her chin as she continued to wave at the audience. She really did love being on the stage, but maybe it was a good thing Ray had signed her up for this. She never would've done it otherwise, and maybe a dinner out with a perfectly normal person was exactly what she needed. Whoever won this auction wouldn't be part of her security team, her manager, or even her mother. It would be someone who could tell her about their daily life and struggles, someone who was real. Despite all her misgivings about it initially, she was actually starting to get a little excited.

"Going once, going twice, sold to number 647 in the front row! Thank you very much, sir. You can head around to the side of the stage to visit our cashier."

Dakota blinked. It was over just as quickly as it had begun. She waved once more as she watched the winner head over to pay. Her heart clenched for a moment as a flicker of doubt passed through her. It was the same doubt she'd had when she'd first been told of the auction: what if her stalker was the one with the winning bid? But this wasn't Rory Black, with his long dark hair. It was a blonde man wearing a short-sleeved button-down and khakis. He looked like he probably sold insurance.

"You're still smiling," Tyler noted when she

joined him once again. They headed down a set of stairs and away from the grandstand.

"I like to think I've made the best out of a bad situation. Or that I've just realized the situation wasn't as bad as I thought it was in the first place. I'll go on this little dinner date, get the concert done, and we'll be on our way out of Wyoming in no time." Her smile started to fade on that last part.

She'd been so eager to get out of Sheridan from the moment she'd arrived. Things were different now that Bryce knew the truth. How many times over these past five years had she wondered if she should tell him? She'd always chosen not to in the end, hoping to protect her son from whoever Bryce might truly be. The way he'd acted the night before had only proven her point. That wild look that Bryce often had in his eyes had changed into something even more dangerous, though Dakota wasn't exactly sure how to explain it. He'd definitely been livid, though. His anger simmered under the surface of his skin, barely controlled, and for once, Dakota had been glad Tyler was within earshot in case she needed to scream for help.

She sighed as they headed back to the bus. A couple of nights of passion had certainly made things complicated.

11

"THANK YOU SO MUCH FOR COMING TO HAVE DINNER with us, Shaw. Can I get you some dessert?" Willa asked as she got up from the dining table.

"That would be great. Thank you again for having me."

"I'll be honest. It's just something I picked up from the bakery. I don't exactly have a lot of time to throw a cheesecake together by hand," she laughed.

"I can't imagine that you do." Shaw gave her a small smile. It only drew up one corner of his mouth, since the scar that ran down his face kept the other side in a grim line. Bryce had almost never seen Shaw even attempt to smile, but it figured that he would direct it at a woman. He had a soft spot for females, and he had a reputation for tossing any man who didn't behave himself right out of the Full Moon Saloon.

Of course, that soft spot made Bryce almost wish they hadn't invited their Alpha over that night. He'd hardly been able to eat over the past day, even though the demanding work of helping to run a ranch usually left him completely famished. He hadn't been able to get over the news he'd confirmed with Dakota, nor the way she felt about him.

"Where's Zane?" Shaw asked as he wiped his hands on his napkin. "I thought maybe you'd called me over here tonight because he was ready to join our pack."

"He hasn't said anything to me about it, but then again, he doesn't say much of anything at all," Willa explained. "He's got a sick aunt in the hospital, so he's been spending a lot of time with her."

"It's a real shame he couldn't be here for all this," Caleb enthused as he dug into his slice of cheese-cake. "He said his aunt is doing poorly and she might not make it through the night."

"I'll be saving a slice for him. God only knows what you boys bother to feed yourselves when we aren't all eating together."

"You can't talk," Colton fired back at his mate

with a grin. "You only had a bowl of cereal for dinner last night."

Willa shot a sour look at him, but her eyes were soft. "I'll have you know I came back downstairs after you fell asleep and ate a huge plate of salami and cheese. I had a sudden craving for protein."

"Sounds like you know how the rest of us feel," Shaw said. "Colton said you're not having any further trouble with your transition." He was watching her carefully, looking for any signs that she might not be feeling well.

Willa had been a human when she'd come to the ranch, but some rather odd events had left her with a bite from a shifter and a new life as one herself. Bryce knew he wasn't privy to the struggles that Colton and Willa experienced as she learned how to embrace this new side of herself, but as far as he could tell, she seemed to be doing just fine. She usually opted for her human form, but Bryce could sense the wolf that now lived in her.

"Yes, thank you," Willa beamed.

Colton cleared his throat. "Shaw, Bryce and I were hoping we could have a chance to talk with you this evening. Privately."

Caleb scraped the last of his cheesecake off his plate. "I'm heading out to work my shift at the pony rides. I'll catch you all later!" With his typical enthusiasm, he headed out the door.

Willa tipped her head toward the kitchen as she gathered the dessert plates. "I'll be washing up."

When it was down to just the three of them, Colton ushered his Alpha and his ranch hand into the living room. "I didn't mean to lure you here under any false pretenses, Shaw, but we've got a situation that can't wait until the next meeting."

"I imagined it was something along those lines," Shaw said in that deep monotone of his. "I know I'm not exactly the most entertaining company."

Bryce sighed, trying to think of how he would put all this to his Alpha without upsetting him. "Bear with me, Shaw. There's a lot to go over. The quick version is that I got a woman pregnant five years ago."

Shaw's brows shot up to his hairline. "You've never mentioned a child. You should know how I feel about people taking care of their own."

"I do. The thing is, I didn't even know about my son until a couple of days ago. I saw the kid from a distance, and I never even imagined he could be mine." Bryce hurried to explain his experience at the pony rides with Kipp.

"I see." Shaw sat back a little on the sofa, silent

for a long moment. "You're a part of this pack, but you hardly ever come to the meetings or participate in any other way. Now you've come to me because you have a problem you don't know how to solve on your own?"

Bryce's heart froze. Shit. Was Shaw just going to leave him in the lurch? "I'm sorry for that. I guess you could say I'm not a pack person."

The corner of Shaw's mouth tugged slightly to the side. "No shit."

Colton snickered behind his hand. He pressed his lips together in an effort to control himself before the Alpha got onto him.

"Take care of the kid. What else is there to decide?"

"Well..." Bryce realized he hadn't exactly explained the entire problem yet. "His mother is Dakota Jones, a human and a rather famous country singer."

"Ah." Shaw's face remained neutral.

"I know how much trouble a young shifter can get into when left to his own devices. I was one myself. I was constantly being thrown back and forth between my parents and the children's home, and I didn't learn to control myself until I got a lot older. I don't want that to happen to Kipp, but I can't help him at all unless I tell Dakota that I'm not human, and neither is her son."

"Don't you think she might understand?" Colton asked. "Willa was a little freaked out when I first told her, but she got past it. You said she's your mate. That connection can make some pretty magical things happen, even when we don't expect it."

"No matter how I feel about the situation, she made it pretty clear that she doesn't want me to be a part of her life or Kipp's. I don't know that I can just let this go, though. I'm not ready to be a dad. I don't know that I ever will be, but how could I just let him be out there in the world without me?" Bryce braced his head in his hands. He felt like he was being torn in half, both emotionally and physically. His wolf cried out for him to bring his newfound family together, but his human side knew that it could only end in disaster.

"You're sure the boy inherited shifter traits?" Shaw asked.

"Yes. I sensed it in him, but it was weak. If I have to guess, I'd say Kipp has no idea what's inside him, and neither does his mother." Would she have told him if she did? Given how little she trusted him, Bryce would guess not. But the entertainment rags would've gotten a hold of that little detail in a hurry, especially when it came to a child who probably wouldn't be able to control himself.

Shaw rubbed a hand down the side of his face. He looked at the floor, but his eyes were distant. "The first thing you need to do is to be absolutely sure. Our feelings often guide us, and in many situations, that's not a bad thing. But if there's even the slightest chance that you're wrong, proceeding with anything further would only be detrimental."

Bryce scrubbed his fingers through his hair. "I'm not sure how I'm going to do that."

"I suggest you find a way," Shaw said firmly. "Once you do know for sure, then you'll have to tell her."

"You're all right with that?" Bryce asked. "I mean, with just coming right out and telling her who we are?" It was a secret that he'd been keeping his entire life. No one had even had to tell him to keep that secret. He'd simply known. He remembered feeling different from the other kids during his stints at the children's home, and in those times, he'd rather be back at home dealing with his drunken father than wondering if a kid would somehow end up figuring him out. He didn't want Kipp to have to experience anything like that.

Shaw tipped his head slightly to the right, a

barely perceptive gesture that suggested a hint of doubt. "It's not something we should consider lightly. If that information were to get into the wrong hands, then it could be a disaster. In this case, though, even if Miss Jones rejects you as a mate, she still has a son with your blood. She'll have to deal with it, and so will we."

Bryce let out a sarcastic laugh. "You know, I've been through some real shit in my life. I've had all sorts of troubles that I've had to figure out, but at a young age, I learned to take it one day at a time. This is freaking me out, though. I don't know how to deal with any of it. Even with you sitting there telling me to do this and do that, it just sounds impossible. I don't know if that makes any sense."

"It makes sense to me," Colton offered. "I think we all grow up thinking that finding our mate will mean we won't have to make any decisions because the universe has already made that decision for us. We think of it as simply falling in love, and that's it. I know it was a lot more complicated than that with Willa, and it felt like a no-win situation. As you can see, though, everything worked out."

"Sure, but she's not a celebrity," Bryce retorted. "Willa is great, and you know I think the world of her, but she's not in the public eye. She didn't flat-out reject you because you aren't up to the standards that her fans want from her. She didn't have to worry about album sales or a bodyguard or a fucking stalker." He slammed his fist against the arm of the chair.

Shaw glanced at that curled fist. "Perhaps she's fighting the same battle within herself that you are," he suggested. "It's not easy to be a parent when you won't see the results of the decisions you make today for another ten or twenty years. Consider that she might also be trying to figure out how she can make it work, but she wants what's best for her child."

"And that's to be without his father?" Bryce's eyes widened a little as soon as the words came out of his mouth. He was practically taking up the torch of being this kid's dad when he hardly even knew him.

That earned him another tweak of Shaw's mouth. "I think you'll get that part figured out. In the meantime, know that you have my blessing to tell her our secret when the time is right and you're absolutely sure it's necessary. I'd better get going. My animals will be wondering where their dinner is." The older man got up and headed out the door.

"Thanks for coming by." Colton followed him, and Bryce could hear him and Willa saying goodbye to their guest.

"Yeah, thanks for nothing," Bryce grumbled

when Colton came back into the living room. "He wasn't that much help."

Colton settled back into his chair and focused his blue eyes on Bryce. "You're only saying that because you didn't like his advice. You'd rather turn in the other direction and run instead of dealing with this."

"Don't accuse me of being a pussy!" Bryce had never felt such sheer anger toward his boss, but something snapped inside him. He shot up out of his chair, feeling the urge to tear something apart. "I'm trying my damnedest to do the right thing here!"

"Right, but that doesn't always mean it's easy," Colton said quietly. He hadn't moved an inch when Bryce jumped up like that, and he still didn't. "You'd rather run in the other direction and not have to deal with it because it's hard. It's making you think about all the things you thought you wanted in your life and how much some of those ideas might have to change. Trust me. I know. Maybe not about the kid part, but definitely about the rest."

Damn him. He was just trying to get Bryce to talk about it. He was no better than Shaw. Then again, Bryce was the one who'd come to them for advice in the first place. Maybe he was the asshole. Actually, he was sure he was, but that still didn't make things any clearer for him. "I just don't know if I can do this," he said as he flopped back down into the chair. "I don't know anything about raising a kid. And how is that supposed to work out with Dakota being in the studio or on the road? And what about my job?"

Colton got up and went to the liquor cabinet. He poured them each a shot of whiskey and handed one to Bryce. "Don't worry about the logistics. That will all work out. You just need to get past the whole part about making sure Kipp is what you think he is and telling Dakota. The rest will come after that."

Bryce knocked back the amber liquid and focused on the fire that it sent snaking down his throat and into his stomach. "I sure as shit hope you're right."

12

"MOM, HAVE YOU SEEN THE HAIR SPRAY?" DAKOTA SET down the curling iron and studied her reflection in the mirror. If she'd been heading for the stage, her hair and makeup would've been amped up. When she was just hanging out on the tour bus, she barely slicked on a bit of mascara and some BB cream. This evening, she'd tried to find a middle ground that would make her look ready for a date without going overboard. Hell, maybe if she enjoyed herself enough, she'd just give up her music career entirely. She could get a job at a restaurant and volunteer with the PTA.

"Oh, here. I used it all, but I bought some more." The rustling of a shopping bag and then footsteps preceded Frankie's appearance in the bathroom doorway. She handed over the can of hairspray and then frowned. "Don't you think you ought to do it up a little more? Maybe some darker lipstick?"

Dakota shot her mom a look. "I was trying to go for something a little more normal."

"The guy is going on a date with a celebrity," Frankie reasoned. "He's not interested in normal. Here, we can just tease the back of your hair a little. It gives a bit of volume, and I think it looks nice with these light curls." She grabbed a comb and lifted her hands.

Dakota stepped back and batted her mother's hand away. "Stop that! I don't want volume. It's fine the way it is."

"Fine, then let's go see what Tyler has to say about it." Frankie gestured toward the living room.

"It doesn't matter what Tyler has to say about it."

"I can hear you." The bodyguard's deep voice rumbled through the bus.

"He can hear you," Frankie echoed. "You ask his opinion on lots of other things, and I don't see a reason why your hair can't be one of them." She took Dakota by the elbow.

"She also rejects my opinion on a lot of things," Tyler said.

"You only want his opinion because you think he'll side with you," Dakota pointed out.

"There now." Frankie had dragged Dakota out into the living area, and she made a grand gesture to present her daughter to the bodyguard sitting in the chair. "What do you think?"

Dakota rolled her eyes. "Mom, it doesn't matter what he thinks!"

Tyler shrugged. "I think you could use a little more volume."

"I think it doesn't matter what you think because you aren't going on this outing with me anyway," Dakota finally spat out.

The bodyguard's eyebrows shot up and then came down so low she could barely see his eyes. "And when were you planning to tell me this?"

"I was hoping to wait as long as possible, because I knew you wouldn't like the idea. But hear me out," she continued quickly before he could tell her just how much he didn't like it. "When I was at that auction, I realized how nice it could be to go on what's essentially a blind date. That's the most non-celebrity thing I've done in years. I don't even get to buy my own groceries anymore unless I want to get cornered for autographs in the produce section. I want this to be as normal as possible, and normal people don't have bodyguards lurking over their shoulders."

"I don't lurk." Tyler glowered at the laptop screen in front of him.

Kipp, who'd been coloring on the floor near the front of the bus, turned around to see what was going on. "I think you look pretty, Mommy!"

"Thank you, baby." Of course, Kipp would say that even if her hair was stringy and she didn't have any makeup on, but she still appreciated the compliment.

"Honey, can I talk to you for a minute?" Frankie dragged Dakota toward the back of the bus until they were in the master suite. She shut the door behind her. "I think you and I should talk."

"If my hair is that important to you, then I'll change it." Dakota felt a knot of nerves in her stomach. Her mom hadn't pulled her aside for a private conversation in years, probably not since she was pregnant with Kipp.

"It's not that. You do whatever you want with your hair, dear. I try to give you my honest opinion on things, but at the end of the day, these are your decisions. I'm just along for the ride, and I fully acknowledge that."

Dakota sat on the end of the bed. "Don't say that, Mom. You're making me feel bad."

"No, honey. You don't understand. I don't just mean about your career or even being here on tour with you." Frankie sat next to Dakota and gently touched one of her daughter's fresh curls. "That's something I had to learn to accept a very long time ago. When you were fifteen and you started hanging out in parking lots with other kids on the weekends, or when you were driving at sixteen and I couldn't always know where you were and that you were safe. A person has to learn to make their own decisions and to live with the consequences, and I knew I couldn't just live your life for you for the first eighteen years and then turn you out into the world and expect you to know what to do. So I've been trying hard not to get too involved."

"But?" It was a sweet sentiment, and Dakota knew that someday she'd have to come to similar terms with Kipp. Still, she knew there was more coming.

"I can't help thinking you're making a big mistake tonight, one that might have bigger consequences than you realize. I know I can't make you do anything you want to do, but this stalker has me worried."

"There's nothing to worry about. I've thought about this a lot. I know there's a certain risk to it, but this guy and I will be in public the entire time. I'm meeting him at the restaurant, so we're arriving and leaving separately. And he looks perfectly harmless. It'll be fine. I can even take the PR perspective on this and say that I think people will actually think it's neat that I'm willing to get out and rub elbows with regular people." Dakota really had spent a lot of time thinking about it. She didn't want to do anything stupid, but it all seemed so foolproof.

Frankie rubbed her lips together. "Are you getting a little burned out, sweetie? Because you know we could talk to Ray about cutting back your tour or and getting some time off."

Dakota sighed. "I love what I do. I love writing and recording music, and even performing. I love being onstage and seeing how much my songs can move my fans. It's the rest of it that's hard and leaves me wishing things were different. Other people clock out at the end of the day and get actual time off work, but I don't feel like I ever do."

"I understand," Frankie nodded. "Here's a suggestion: Let Tyler go with you tonight, but once you're through with your current commitments, you take some real time off work. We can go on a vacation, maybe to some other country where no one's ever heard of you before. Then you can be 'normal.' But for tonight, I still think you're Dakota Jones: Superstar." She fanned out her hands for emphasis.

"It's a nice thought, Mom, but I really want to do this." She looked up when a knock sounded on the door. "Come in."

Tyler slid the door aside, looking even more irritated than before. "That guy Bryce is here to talk to you again. I can send him away and tell him you're busy." His mouth was a hard line.

Dakota had already been a little nervous about this date, and she wasn't sure she wanted to deal with Bryce right now. He was probably just going to bitch her out again for not telling him the truth. She opened her mouth to tell Tyler to send Bryce in, but then she thought about Kipp. "I'll come out." She ignored the look of interest on Frankie's face as she got up.

Stepping off the bus, she found herself face-to-face with Bryce once again. "Hey."

"Hi. What are you all dolled up for?" He raked his eyes down the brown and teal maxi dress she'd paired with tall cowboy boots and a squash blossom necklace. Bryce wasn't dressed up at all in his usual t-shirt and jeans, yet she found herself wishing he was the one who'd come to pick her up for a date.

"I have a thing I have to go to." Dakota silently chided herself for being secretive. What did it matter if he knew she had a charity dinner date? It was probably all over the internet and the news, anyway.

"Well, um, maybe that works out, actually." He skimmed a hand over his shaved head. "I was wondering if...I mean, I wanted to ask you about..." Bryce paused and let out a sigh. "I wanted to spend some time with Kipp."

"Oh, Bryce." Her shoulders sank and her stomach spun. This was what she'd been trying to avoid. "I don't think it's a good idea. We'll be leaving in a few days."

"And that's exactly why I want to do it," he urged. "I can't just send him off on the road without trying to get to know him. At least then, if someday you decide you want to let him know, then he might look back and know that I actually took the time to hang out with him when I had the chance."

Dakota bit her lip, feeling unsure. It seemed like a simple enough request, but she was protective of her son.

"Please, Dakota." His eyes were dark honey as he looked at her. "I'm not going to say anything to him. I'll just be your friend and the guy from the pony rides. Nothing more, not unless you think it's okay."

Would it hurt? Could she trust him to do as he said? Damn it, this was hard. This would be the only time that Kipp would meet his father, considering they'd be heading out before too long. "And you won't say anything?"

"Not a thing. I swear it."

He was so solemn, so earnest. Even that wildfire that was always burning in his eyes was somewhat subdued. "Give me a second, okay?"

"Of course."

Feeling his eyes burning into her back, Dakota stepped back onto the bus. "Kipp, I have something I want to ask you."

"What is it?" Kipp left his crayons on the floor as he got up and came over to her. "Are you sad?"

"No, honey. I'm fine," she lied. Dakota had already found that parenting often involved lying simply to protect him, but how much longer could she keep up the façade? When, as Frankie had to do, would she have to let Kipp know the truth and make his own decisions? He was young, but at least in this moment, it seemed that he should have a say. "Do you remember my friend Bryce? The one with the drawings on his arms that was running the pony rides?"

"Yeah!"

"Well..." She trailed off as she saw that both Frankie and Tyler were watching her. They would probably understand all the implications that came with what she was about to say, even if Kipp didn't. Oh, well. Dakota wasn't sure how long she could keep the lid on this anyway. "He's here, and he was wondering if you'd like to spend some time with him."

"What are we going to do?" Kipp asked excitedly. "I've got to find my shoes!"

"I guess that's a yes," Dakota muttered to herself. "I'm not sure, honey. We'll have to ask him."

Kipp was on his hands and knees, digging a sneaker out from under the sofa. "Can you help me tie this?"

"Of course I can, buddy." Her heart broke with every pull and tug of his laces. Kipp was just a little boy, completely innocent. It wasn't his fault that he was the result of a wild tryst between a singer and a ranch hand that never should've happened in the first place. She worried so much about all the decisions she made for Kipp and how they would turn out in the end, and she hoped like hell that this wouldn't be one she would regret.

Only a minute later, they were heading back outside. Kipp immediately ran over to Bryce, who held out his hand for a high-five. His fingers looked so small and soft compared to the large, rugged ones on Bryce. He was grinning ear-to-ear, looking more excited than Dakota had seen him in a few days. When she glanced up, she saw that Bryce was smiling, too.

She lifted her chin slightly in the air, hoping to let him know that he might've won this round, but she was still the one in charge. "Where do you plan to go?"

Bryce scratched the back of his neck. "The park, I think. Maybe we'll grab a bite to eat if he gets hungry."

"Let me give you my cell number. For emergencies," she clarified quickly.

"Right. Of course."

Dakota could feel an energy between herself and Bryce, but she wasn't sure how to identify it. She wanted to go with them, to go run around the park and get hamburgers and milkshakes afterward. The thing was, she couldn't tell if she wanted to do that so she could keep an eye on them, or because she genuinely wanted to be part of the fun. It felt like she was missing out on something. "You be good, Kipp. Mind your manners."

"I will, Mommy! Bye!" As though he'd known Bryce his entire life, Kipp slipped his hand into Bryce's, ready to leave.

Dakota caught the stiffening of Bryce's shoulders for a moment before they took off. She smiled a little to herself. It was amusing to see a grown man intimidated by a little boy. She was far less amused, however, when she got back on the bus. Frankie was standing there near the door with her arms folded across her chest and a pensive look across her face.

"Are you sure about this?" she asked. She tipped her head slightly forward, implying that she understood exactly what was going on.

Dakota glanced out the window, where she just caught Bryce and Kipp disappearing between two horse trailers. "It'll be fine. Kipp will be safe with him."

Frankie fiddled with an earring, a leather tassel with a silver thunderbird. "I guess that's not really what I mean..."

"I know what you mean." Dakota glanced at Tyler, wondering what he was going to have to say about all this, but he was hiding behind the local newspaper. "I did what I thought was right, Mom."

"I can respect that," Frankie said genuinely. There were still many questions in her eyes, but she didn't press the issue any further. "I guess that means I have the afternoon off. I think I spotted a day spa downtown. I could use a pedicure and a massage."

Dakota noted that her mother didn't look all that pleased about having time to herself. She tried to take that as a good thing, though. It meant Frankie didn't mind the job she'd taken up of being Kipp's onboard nanny. "That sounds like a nice idea. How about you, Tyler? Looks like you've got some time to yourself, too."

He put down his paper. The bodyguard always had a fairly stoic visage, but he looked uncomfortable. "I haven't decided yet."

"You can come get a pedicure with me," Frankie offered. "I promise I won't tell anyone."

"No, thanks," Tyler replied quickly. "Maybe I'll just get out and see the touristy things. Or go watch some of the rodeo."

"Sounds good." Dakota wouldn't be surprised at all if Tyler just sat right where he was and shopped for security cameras on the internet. There was always a chance he would go ahead and follow her to her date, too. Dakota decided not to worry about it as she checked her watch. "Looks like it's time for me to go. I'll see you guys later."

She gripped the wheel of their rental car, trying to remember the last time she drove herself somewhere. But Dakota was far more worried about how things were going with Kipp and Bryce.

13

KIPP TAPPED HIS FINGER AGAINST HIS CHIN AS HE studied the pictures on the side of the ice cream truck, trying to decide what to get. "I don't like that one. I had that one once."

"Do you like chocolate?" Bryce pointed out a fudge bar. "Or ice cream sandwiches?"

"Oh, yeah! An ice cream sandwich! The kind with the cookies!" Kipp jumped up and down, nearly screaming his delight.

"Good choice. One ice cream sandwich and one sundae cone." Bryce fiddled with the cash in his wallet. Getting some cheap treats from a truck wasn't a big deal, but everything about Kipp made him nervous. He worried that he would make the wrong impression on the kid, and then of course, Kipp would tell his mother.

Bryce didn't want to admit that he was still holding out on a chance with Dakota. She was so far above him, and that in itself would just make things difficult. Then there was the fact that she was a human, and she'd probably be less than thrilled if she found out what Bryce was. *When,* he reminded himself, because he had no real reason to doubt that he'd be telling her soon enough.

He couldn't deny that he was still pissed at her, though. Dakota had purposely kept their son a secret from him. She never would've admitted it at all if he hadn't figured it out. Bryce had every right to be angry and to erase any thoughts of her from his mind, but his wolf always seemed to have other plans.

"There's a bench over there where we can sit down." Bryce took the treats and led the way. A wave of warmth washed over his chest when Kipp climbed up next to him and sat down so close that their legs were touching. The kid liked him. How about that?

"This is good!" Kipp said around a mouthful of ice cream. "Do you like yours?"

"I do." Bryce bit into the peanuts and chocolate

at the top and chewed, but he wasn't paying attention to the ice cream at all. This entire outing had merely been a ruse to get closer to the kid and make absolutely sure he was a shifter. He'd already gotten the confirmation he needed before they even got in the truck. Bryce could sense the wolf in him. It was far below the surface, quiet and recessed, but it was definitely there. Still, he hadn't been lying when he said he wanted a chance to spend time with Kipp before they left. Depending on how this all went, he might never see Kipp again. His heart twisted like a damp rag at the thought.

"Do you have to work at the pony rides today?" Kipp asked.

"No, not today. Someone else is doing it for me."

"Do you like the pony rides?" Kipp licked the ice cream on the edge of his sandwich before nibbling at the cookie.

Should he answer that honestly? Bryce didn't want to lie to him, but he couldn't exactly say how much he loathed having to lift a bunch of snot-nosed kids in and out of the saddle. Kipp would think he meant him, and he definitely didn't. "It's not too bad, but I prefer to be working out on the ranch with the other cowboys."

"What do you do?" Kipp swung his legs back and

forth underneath the bench, bouncing a little with the effort.

"A lot of things. We all herd the cattle and help make sure they stay healthy. We have a lot of buildings and fences that we have to make sure are in good shape, so sometimes we have to fix those. And we have to make sure the predators stay away from the cattle. You know, wolves and things." He knew he was pushing it. He was being too hopeful that the mere mention of a wolf would give him some sort of definitive proof.

"I'm a wolf!" Kipp exclaimed. "I like to run around and howl at the moon and eat sheep!"

Bryce almost choked on his sundae cone, but then he realized what was happening. Kipp was just playing pretend, but was there a reason that wolves were part of his imaginary world? Probably, and the kid had no idea. "Really? Well, it sounds like you're a very busy wolf indeed. Do you know any other wolves?"

"No, but that's okay. I don't have to." Kipp polished off his ice cream sandwich and crumpled the wrapper in his hand. He pointed to the jungle gym, where several other children were playing and laughing. "Can I go over there and play?"

"Sure. I'll throw your wrapper away." Bryce

accepted the trash and watched as Kipp took off at top speed for the playground. He immediately climbed up onto the jungle gym, his little hands and feet flying as he went up the ladder. Standing in line behind some other children waiting to use the slide, he began talking to another little boy.

Bryce let out a long breath through his nose. He couldn't exactly fault Dakota for the way she raised the boy. He could easily have been a spoiled rotten brat as the child of a celebrity, but he was sweet, curious, and genuine. He was also, without a doubt, a shifter.

"He's a good kid, isn't he?" a voice said a little ways behind him.

Bryce turned to see Tyler standing near the fence that surrounded the playground. He was dressed in a t-shirt and jeans, a contrast from the suit and sunglasses that he usually had on when he was actively guarding Dakota. Just knowing that this man had been assigned to protect his mate made Bryce curdle a little inside, but he wasn't about to let it show.

He strolled over. "I guess you were sent here to babysit me?" he asked casually.

"Not at all," Tyler said with a shake of his head. "I just wanted to talk. You and I are a lot alike."

Bryce watched him carefully. He could sense the bear inside the man. It was massive, and it could put up one hell of a fight if it needed to, but it was quiet at the moment. "We are."

"And so is that young man out there." Tyler nodded toward the playground. "I think you already know that, though."

Well, this was an interesting turn of events. Bryce grappled with how to handle it. He was used to operating alone. He figured things out for himself, and he didn't go running to anyone for help. Now he'd already gone to Colton and Shaw, which had been unusual enough. It felt like a complete betrayal of who he was as a person to discuss this with Tyler, too, but he had to admit that the bodyguard had insight on the people Bryce was most interested in. "I do. I sensed it before, but I had to make sure I was right. I take it he hasn't gone through his first shift."

"What makes you think I would know?" Tyler said evasively.

Bryce leveled his gaze at him. "I get the feeling you know a lot."

"Sometimes more than I like to admit. Anyway, no. He hasn't. I've worried about that time a lot, because I know it'll come eventually. The boy has no idea what he really is or that people like us exist. Between his very human upbringing and the fact that Dakota gives him a lot of room to express himself freely, I don't expect it to come any time soon. It'll take something big, like a traumatic event. Or puberty, which is traumatic enough." He let out a gruff laugh as he glanced over at the kids on the playground.

Numerous questions hovered on the tip of Bryce's tongue. He thought it would be best to clear the air with the one that would help him establish exactly who was who in this whole situation. "Is there something going on between you and Dakota?"

Tyler's dark eyes were hard as stone when he glanced at Bryce. "No. It's not like that at all. This isn't the movies, man. Some of us are just trying to do our jobs. Not that I don't care about her, just as I do Kipp and Frankie, it's just not like that."

"Then why are you here talking to me about all this?" Bryce pressed. He was like a dog with a bone now. He had to get down to all the nitty-gritty details, whether he liked them or not. His window of opportunity was getting smaller and smaller because it was obvious Dakota wasn't going to stick around in Sheridan any longer than she had to. "You could just as easily let me figure it all out on my own and make an ass of myself."

"Oh, I think you'll do a good enough job of that on your own." The corner of Tyler's mouth quirked up, and he shook his head. "I see what's in your eyes when you look at Dakota. I know this isn't just some crush."

Bryce wiped a hand over his mouth. He knew what he felt. That bond he'd established with her so long ago had been nagging at the back of his mind for years, making him wonder what would have happened if he'd made different decisions. It drove him crazy when he was near her, and sometimes it drove him even crazier when he couldn't be near her. He'd never imagined, though, that someone else would be able to see it on his face, plain as day. "No. Not exactly."

"I didn't know anything about Kipp's father until we rolled into Sheridan. Dakota had kept that information to herself, and I didn't ask. It wasn't my place to. But even before this week, I've been concerned for Kipp and what's going to happen to him once he understands that he's not just playing pretend when he says he's a wolf. He's going to get the shit scared out of him, and he's going to scare the shit out of a lot of other people. Including Dakota."

"So she has no idea," Bryce confirmed. He'd already been fairly sure of that, but it was nice to get a little insight. He watched as Kipp and another boy started playing tag around the jungle gym, grinning and laughing without a care in the world.

"Not a clue. I always figured I'd have to make sure I could stick around long enough so that I could be there for Kipp when the time came. I might not know how it is to be a wolf, but a shifter is a shifter. I wanted to help. But I think you might be a better help than I am."

"That's awfully good of you, considering he's not your kid," Bryce pointed out. Damn. Tyler was just a hired man, but he was already a much better father than Bryce could even imagine being. He knew he wanted to be there to protect Kipp and do more for him than his own dad had, but that was about it.

"He's not, but he's family as far as I'm concerned. They all are. The thing is, I think there's someone much more qualified to help him out," Tyler said pointedly.

"I'm not so sure about that." Bryce looked over at his son once again. His son. That was a hard one to wrap his head around. If it weren't for the wolf pup inside the boy, he could easily believe he belonged to someone else. There was no doubt that he was

Dakota's, though, not with those looks. "I think you're forgetting how incompatible Dakota and I are. She doesn't want to have anything to do with me, and she wants me to stay out of Kipp's life." He couldn't keep the resentment out of his voice.

Tyler thoughtfully rubbed a hand through the thick stubble on his jawline. "Dakota has been working really hard to strike the right balance in her life. She wants her career. She loves it. The music is important to her, and it drives her forward when she can tell how much her fans get into it. The thing is, she also wants a normal life. Not just for Kipp—although there's definitely that—but for herself, too. She likes being on the stage, but she doesn't want to be in the spotlight when she's just going for a walk."

"I guess she must really appreciate that stalker then, huh?" Bryce said it lightly, but he knew how he felt about it. If he had the chance, he'd take any man who tried to come near her and rip him right in half.

"Then there's that," Tyler said with a nod. "It makes my job damn hard when she needs security but doesn't want me 'lurking' over her shoulder." He crooked his fingers in the air to make quotes.

Bryce pressed his lips together, not wanting to come right out and laugh. He could easily imagine

Dakota putting the bodyguard in his place. "I'm sure."

"The bottom line is, whether Dakota realizes it or not, her son is going to be quite the attention-getter when the time comes. She's going to need a shifter around to help them both through it. That could be a hired man who cares very much, or it could be her mate and the father of her child."

The words hit Bryce like a blow to the chest. Even though he had Shaw's permission to reveal their secret, he'd still been ready to just turn the other way. It was too much responsibility, and he didn't know if he was up for the task. But Tyler was right. Dakota needed him. "That's certainly something to think about."

Just then, Kipp broke away from his new friends and came running over. "Bryce, will you push me in the swing? Hi, Tyler! You want to play with us?"

Tyler smiled down at him. "No thanks, kid. I just stopped by to say hi. I'll see you back on the bus."

"Okay. Bye!" Kipp was off and running again.

Bryce nodded at Tyler. "Looks like I've got to go. I'll see you around."

"See ya."

As he pushed the little boy on the swings, Bryce wished his life could be as simple as Kipp's.

14

"MA'AM, YOUR GUEST HAS ARRIVED," THE MANAGER said as he held out a chair for the blonde man who'd followed him to the back of the restaurant. His eyes glittered as they raked over her, taking in every detail.

Dakota was used to it, but that didn't mean she liked it. She knew she was just like any other person, yet she'd already seen the manager about six times since she'd arrived. He'd personally brought her a menu and a glass of water, and he'd come back several more times to make sure she had enough to drink, to offer a bottle of champagne on the house, and to let her know he would tell her right away when her dinner date arrived. She wouldn't have been surprised if he'd also offered to run away into the sunset with her.

"Thank you." She stood up and reached out her hand. "It's nice to meet you. I'm Dakota Jones."

"Robert Barnes. It's nice to meet you, too." He shook her hand and waited until she was seated again before he took his chair. He was dressed in an Oxford shirt and khakis, and his loafers had been shined. There was something vaguely familiar about his face, but she couldn't quite place the dark eyes or the blonde hair. "I hope I didn't keep you waiting too long."

"Oh, not at all. I got here a little too early, actually. I'm used to getting through thick traffic in big metropolitan areas, so I overestimated the time it took to get here. It's been nice to just sit and look around at the décor, though. I don't always get enough time to stop and smell the roses." Her mind had wandered several times to Kipp, wondering how he and Bryce were getting along. She'd checked her phone and made sure the ringer volume was up, but there was no news.

"I'm sure."

The manager appeared once again. He gave Robert only a cursory glance, keeping his gaze mostly on Dakota. "May I take your order?"

"I'll have the salmon and the asparagus," Dakota replied, noting that he didn't bother to write it down.

"And you, sir?"

"The steak, and I think asparagus as well." Robert handed his menu back and smiled pleasantly at the manager. He looked amused when the man had gone. "I'm pretty sure he has no idea I'm even here. I'll be lucky if he remembers to bring my food."

"I'm sorry," Dakota began.

"No, don't be sorry at all. I fully expected it. I'm just a humble accountant who thought this would be a fun way to donate to his favorite charity. That's how life works," he replied.

Dakota smiled. She'd had so many doubts about this dinner, but so far, she had no complaints. Robert hadn't fawned all over her or asked to have her autograph for every member of his family. She hadn't even been too far off the mark when she'd initially guessed he sold insurance. He'd been about as normal as he could possibly be, and that was exactly what she needed.

"I guess that's true. I just hope you don't mind that the manager put us all the way in the back. It means that no one can see us together. I'm sorry. That sounds very arrogant of me, to assume you'd want everyone in town to see that you're with me."

She blushed and looked down at her hands. It was easy enough to turn on that celebrity attitude when she was walking down a red carpet at an awards show or taking the stage in front of thousands of fans, but it wasn't the same when she was just at a table in a restaurant. It was like there were two sides of her, and she didn't know how to balance them.

"Don't be sorry at all." Her guest was more than gracious. "I'm not worried about my social status. Everyone in town knows I won that auction, so I think it's safe to say they know what I'm doing tonight whether I have any proof or not."

"Here you are!" the manager announced as he arrived with their plates, and he gently glided Dakota's in front of her with a flourish. "The salmon and asparagus for you, ma'am. I made sure to select the most choice cut myself. Your steak, sir."

"Thank you." It embarrassed Dakota all over again to see him salivating over her like that and treating Robert as though he was nothing, but she decided not to apologize for it again. She couldn't spend the whole meal doing nothing but saying she was sorry. "This looks delicious. Why don't you tell me a bit about yourself?"

"Oh, there's not much to tell. I'm an accountant, as I mentioned. I like to read, and every now and then, I watch a little TV. I'm a bachelor, so I do end up with a bit of free time on my hands. That's when I like to take a hike or go camping."

"Really? That's wonderful." She was about to say he didn't look at all like a man who enjoyed the outdoors, but then she noticed he was cutting his steak with hands that were far more rugged than an accountant would likely have. "It's hard these days, but I do my best to get out into nature when I get the chance, especially with my son. He loves the outdoors. At some point, I'd like to figure out how I can get him into Boy Scouts even though we're on the road so much. I think he could really benefit from it."

"You don't think he'll have a hard time fitting in with the other students, with having a famous mom and everything?" Robert gazed pleasantly at her over the table.

Dakota relaxed a little more into her seat. Even once she'd convinced herself that this dinner was just the thing she needed in her life, she'd worried that whoever had put in the highest bid would spend all their time flattering her. Robert's question could've just as easily come from a friend with genuine concern for her life instead of a fan.

"I think he would be just fine, actually. He's a

great kid, and none of this life has gone to his head. Of course, I'd like to give him as much of a typical childhood as possible. Sometimes Kipp and I even sneak off the tour bus at night to catch fireflies or watch for shooting stars. He's so interested in everything, and I want to feed that as much as I can."

Robert nodded, listening closely as he ate. "And what about your music? Does your son enjoy it as much as your fans do?"

"Not exactly," Dakota said with a laugh. She felt her face getting warm as she talked about Kipp. He'd been the one constant in her life other than her mother. Even Tyler, as reliable as he was, had only fairly recently become a part of her world. Her son meant absolutely everything to her, and she knew that would be the case whether she was a recording artist or a real estate agent. "In fact, when I'm working on a song and I keep playing the same parts over and over, he puts his hands over his ears and whines about how I'm interrupting his cartoons. I always know I can go to him whenever I need a truly honest opinion."

"Kids will be kids," Robert acknowledged. "I don't have any myself, but I'd like to someday. Especially if it was with the right person."

As they ate, their conversation wandered all

over the map. Robert told Dakota about his nieces, his accounting agency, and how he dabbled a bit in music himself. He held off from trying to email her a demo, and Dakota shared what life was like on the road, how she'd managed to go from barely getting gigs at empty bars to filling stadiums, and what her favorite songs were. All in all, it wasn't bad. She couldn't say that she clicked with Robert, and she wouldn't be giving him her email address so they could keep up communication, but it was really nice to feel like she was a part of the real world instead of just looking in on it from time to time.

Robert polished off his steak and slid his plate to the edge of the table. "Will you be up for dessert? They have a great chocolate mousse here."

Dakota frowned at the last few bites that were on her plate. The food had been simply amazing. Her mother did a great job cooking for them, and she was grateful that she wasn't stuck with drive-thru fare all the time, but the salmon had truly been delectable. Of course, chocolate mousse sounded fantastic, too. "Sure. I haven't had that in forever."

"I'm sure the manager will be more than happy to serve it to you on a silver platter and chuck mine in my lap," Robert laughed.

"I sure hope not! That would be quite the waste of good mousse!"

His face grew somber as he studied her. "You're a brave soul to do a charity dinner for an auction with a stranger."

Dakota pushed her plate away, sure that she couldn't possibly eat another bite even though the food was incredible. "Why do you say that? It's been very nice, and I like the idea of helping out a charity." She rested her forearms on the table and folded her hands.

Robert nodded. "It has been nice, and I like to support the animal shelter in any way I can. But I've seen the rumor in the entertainment tabloids about you having a stalker. I don't exactly see you running around with a full security team at your back. That could be very dangerous." He leaned forward and rested his hands on the table just millimeters from hers.

Her back stiffened at the mention of her stalker. Everyone seemed quite happy to bring it up and throw it in her face, particularly when they wanted to use it as an excuse to keep her contained in some way. Personally, she'd rather not think about it at all. "I did have someone who was trying to get close to me, but it's already been taken care of."

"You never know," he said quietly, thoughtfully. His eyes were dull as he reached out with his thumb and grazed the back of her knuckles. "They could be closer than you think."

Dakota jerked her hands off the table. It felt as though Robert's touch had left something physical on her skin, and she badly wanted to scrub it off on a napkin or run to the bathroom. Instead, she threw her hand in the air to signal for the manager.

He came scuttling right over. "Yes, ma'am? What can I do for you?"

"I'd like the check, please."

Robert, who had been all pleasantries and softness, now had a hard look in his eyes. "I thought you wanted dessert."

Damn it. She'd said that. And now this douche would probably throw some sort of fit over the fact that she didn't want to share chocolate fucking mousse with him. Too damn bad. There was something in the air that she didn't like, and it wasn't helped at all by the eager face of the manager as he waited for her to tell him what to do. "I'm afraid I simply can't eat anymore, and I have some things I need to do this evening. I'll take the check."

"As you wish." The manager hurried off.

"I hope I didn't do anything to upset you," Robert

said evenly. His hands were fists on his edge of the table.

At least they weren't anywhere near hers. Dakota had often thought of herself as a huggy, touchy-feely person. She loved to hug her friends and family, and it was nice to be physically close. But a stranger touching her without her permission was completely different, and she couldn't wait to get back and take a long shower. "No. Not at all. It's just that I've realized I've got to get back."

"Right. To your son."

"Yes." She practically threw her credit card at the manager as soon as he arrived, and she was already rising out of her chair before he could even return with the receipt. "I'm sorry I've had to keep this short. I do have a busy schedule. I'm sure you understand."

Snagging her receipt and her card, Dakota hurried out to the car. A shiver ran down her spine, despite the warm air. It felt like someone was staring her down from behind, and she couldn't get back fast enough.

15

THERE WERE MANY TIMES IN DAKOTA'S LIFE WHEN THE tour bus didn't feel like home. It just wasn't the same as her mom's little house in Texas, with her cow skulls on the wall and the quilt her grandmother had made draped over the back of the couch. It didn't help matters that the bus was her office as well as her hotel, so she never really felt like she was getting off work at the end of the day. Tonight, though, she was infinitely grateful to step into the cool air conditioning of the living room.

Kipp was playing with his toy trucks, making them zoom over the back of the couch, down the arms, and across the rug. "Hi, Mommy!"

"Hi, sweetie." She'd never felt so relieved to see

him in her entire life. She hadn't been all that worried that Bryce would do anything crazy, but she sure as hell hoped he'd kept his word and their secret. "Hey, Mom."

"How did it go?" Frankie's voice echoed as she leaned against the counter to poke her head into a cabinet. "And have you seen the Tums? I stopped off for a spicy chicken sandwich and I'm seriously regretting it."

"We might be out."

"Well, that's my luck. There's a convenience store across the street. I'll try there, but otherwise, I'll have to find a pharmacy. I'll never sleep tonight if I don't get this to simmer down. Kipp has already had dinner, by the way. Bryce said they got some burgers before he came back."

"That's good." Dakota felt dryness in her throat hearing her mother speak of Bryce as though he was simply a part of their family. "What about Tyler? Is he around?"

"No, he said he had some things he wanted to do. I didn't ask him what."

Good. That meant Dakota could put off telling him how creepy her charity date had been. It would only prove him right that she should've allowed him to come with her, and she didn't want to hear it from him. At least not right then, when she was still freshly freaked out about the incident. It had been disturbing enough that he'd touched her hand that way, but there was something in his eyes right before she left that she simply didn't like. It was as though Robert Barnes had put on a good attitude like a well-fitting mask, but he'd dropped it as soon as he'd realized things weren't going his way. On the drive back to the fairgrounds, Dakota realized Robert had said he'd donated to the animal shelter. The charity auction had benefitted the children's home. He could simply have misspoken, or he could be a complete liar. Shit. She'd have to tell Tyler.

"You okay, honey?" Frankie had picked up her purse, but she was looking at Dakota with concern.

"I'm fine. I'm just tired. I think I'm going to make some hot tea. I've got to keep my throat ready for tomorrow night." She picked up the kettle and lifted the lid to fill it.

"I know there's some chamomile in the cabinet. I just saw it. I'll be back in a bit."

Dakota put the kettle on the burner and sat on the couch near Kipp. "How was your day, buddy?"

"It was great!" he enthused. "We went to the

park, and there was an ice cream truck! And he told me I could get anything I wanted!"

She raised an eyebrow. "So you had ice cream before dinner?"

Kipp's eyes widened a little. "Yeah, but it was really good! And I still ate all my hamburger!"

"I'll bet you did, sweetie. What else did you do?" So far, everything sounded completely ordinary. As much as Dakota had been craving that sense of normalcy, maybe Kipp had as well. Dakota tried so hard to keep his feet on the ground. It wasn't too hard while he was young, but what would happen once he was in school? Or when he became a teenager? While she could give him a loving, happy childhood wherever they were and whatever they were doing, it was going to get harder and harder to keep him from turning into an entitled brat. She just wanted what was best for him, and she wasn't sure if she was doing it.

The boy shrugged a little. "We played on the playground, and he pushed me in the swing."

Dakota lifted Kipp's shirt sleeve. "No tattoos? No piercings?" She tickled his belly.

Kipp laughed as he rolled away, and Dakota followed him down onto the floor. They tickled and giggled, and Dakota fell in love all over again with her sweet son. She loved the moments like this, and they didn't happen often enough. By the time the tea kettle whistled, she had tears leaking from the corners of her eyes from laughing so hard.

"Hang on, bud. I've got to get this." Swiping a finger under her eye, Dakota knew she was going to have to change her schedule. She wanted more chances to be like that with Kipp, when they could just be themselves and she wasn't rushing out the door.

She found the honey and poured a generous spoonful into the bottom of the mug while she thought about how she might make that happen. Her mother had already suggested a break, and maybe she was right. But how would Ray feel about that? He was just going to push her right back into the studio. There had to be a good balance somewhere.

"Kipp, I've still got plenty of hot water here," she said as she added a tea bag. "Do you want some hot chocolate or something? Kipp?" Dakota snapped her head to the side when there was no response. Kipp's trucks were still there on the floor. The big dump truck was pushed halfway under the front of the couch, and a car hauler had been loaded down with Lightning McQueen and several Hot Wheels. But there was no sign of her son.

Her heart thundered, and adrenaline shook her veins. Dakota had only stepped into the kitchen for a moment, and it wasn't like they were ever far away from each other while they were staying on the tour bus. It might be a large RV, but it was still an RV. "Kipp?"

She breathed a sigh of relief when she saw an oddly shaped lump beneath the throw blanket someone had left on the recliner. "Hmm, I wonder where my Kipp has gone. I miss him so much, and I was hoping I could give him a really big hug."

The blanket didn't giggle in response. He was getting better at this. "Or maybe I'll just tickle him to little pieces when I find him!" Dakota grabbed the corner of the blanket and whisked it aside. But there was no Kipp to come bursting out, only a couple of throw pillows.

"Kipp! Where are you?" Dakota checked the driver's seat and under the table. "This isn't funny, okay?" She slid open the bathroom door and swished the shower curtain aside. Still no Kipp. The smaller sleeping areas were clear, and there was no sign of him in the master suite at the back of the bus.

True panic began overtaking her system. Her heart was pounding inside her skull now as she began to imagine the absolute worst. There was still a bit of logic left in her terrified brain, trying to remind her that Kipp was probably okay. But never in her life had she lost Kipp before. She'd always known precisely where he was or who he was with, at least in general terms. "Kipp!"

With no further places to look on the bus, Dakota scrambled down the stairs and out the door. She swung her head from side to side, her eyes desperately searching the campers, horse trailers, and trucks. She became more and more distressed when she didn't see him looking at his reflection in a side mirror or trying to see if he could climb up the ladder on the back of an RV. He wasn't even trying to point to a tire and say it needed more air as if he actually knew about those sorts of things. "Kipp!"

"I'm back here, Mommy!"

That precious voice sent a stream of relief through her body. The adrenaline began to drain away as she trotted around to the back of the bus, leaving her muscles limp with exhaustion and relief. She began working up a good lecture for her boy about making sure he checked with her before going outside.

The light poles illuminated the front of the bus as she rounded it, but the trees they were parked next to made for dark shadows out behind it. It was a relief to have that natural shade during the day, but it was as black as ink right now. "Kipp, you scared me," she said as she charged into the murkiness. "You can't just leave the bus like that."

"Look, Mommy!"

As her eyes slowly adjusted to the gloom, Dakota saw Kipp's face softly illuminated by a pale green glow. He was grinning, but his face disappeared as the glow moved closer to her. Kipp was holding out his hand to show her. "I see. You caught some fireflies." She pressed her fingers to her temple, hoping to keep her temper and calmly explain to her son how he should've told her he wanted to go out and catch bugs. The fireflies were their little fun routine, a way for them to get away from the world for a moment. She didn't want to ruin that, but she couldn't simply let him get away with this.

"Yeah! And I made a new friend!"

"We can talk about the firefly's name later, Kipp."

"No, not the firefly. My friend. His name is Robert."

Dakota's throat constricted. Her eyes were adjusting further to the darkness, and she no longer needed the glow of the lightning bugs to see that there was a man standing right next to her son. His blonde hair was a little disheveled now, and the way it hung over his ear let her know that it wasn't his actual hair at all. Dakota didn't know how she hadn't noticed before, but she had no time to dwell on her dinner date's appearance. "Robert," she said as she slowly moved closer. "Or should I say, Rory Black?"

16

BRYCE LEANED HEAVILY ON THE FENCE. THE grandstands were packed for the bull riding competition, as they were every year. Everyone wanted to see their favorite rodeo heroes last for the entire eight seconds, but they were also there to witness when things went wrong, as they just had. The rider had started well, but he'd lost control after a few seconds and went pitching off the front of the bull. His body had barely skimmed the horns, saving him from getting gored. The audience had breathed a collective sigh of relief, but that quickly turned into screams once again. The cowboy was scrambling to get to his feet, but the bull sought revenge on the man who'd dared to ride him. He leveled his horns and charged. The rodeo clowns were on it, though, springing into action and luring the bull away while the rider clambered over the fence to safety.

It might be exciting if he was in the right mood for it, but Bryce couldn't focus. He had far too much on his mind to worry about who would last the longest, because he felt like he was riding a wild bull of his own as he decided what to do about Dakota.

If he went and told her the truth about himself and Kipp, she wouldn't believe him. Not until he showed her, anyway, and that probably wouldn't go well. It was hard to imagine that any normal human would just be perfectly okay with such a huge revelation. He'd be bucked off in two seconds flat.

The other option was one that he would've taken in a heartbeat when he was younger, and that was to let Dakota leave without saying a word. He knew Tyler would look out for Kipp, so it was possible to justify the decision with the knowledge that the boy wouldn't be left without help. But what if something happened to Tyler or Dakota decided not to use him as a bodyguard any longer? It sounded like she was always trying to get away from him as it was.

Bryce pushed off the fence and slowly began walking toward the tour bus. It was getting late, and he was going to have to make his decision soon enough. It sounded easy to run away, but there was one huge problem. It meant abandoning both his mate and his son. Bryce knew what he wanted. He could imagine himself finding some way to make their lives work together, and he'd already thought it out in stunningly great detail. The thought of Dakota sharing a bed with him every night and Kipp sleeping in the next room was one that made his wolf curl up in contentment.

He hadn't been able to stop thinking about it from the time he'd dropped Kipp off with Frankie. Bryce had never imagined he'd have such a good time with a five-year-old, but it had genuinely been a fun afternoon. He wanted to share more with the boy than just a little food and time in the park. He wanted to show him what it was like to work on a ranch. He wanted to put him up on a horse—a real horse—and demonstrate that there was really no need to be afraid of any horse if you did the right things to keep yourself safe.

That was all just a fantasy, though, and he knew it. If he really thought about it, there was no way Dakota would ever accept him. She would reject him. Even if she didn't know about his true identity, she'd already made it clear she didn't like him for who he was as a person. Maybe the best thing he could do would be to say goodbye and tell Dakota that he could be there whenever Kipp needed him. Maybe—just maybe—she would call him up when Kipp turned around one day and showed her that he wasn't just a simple human after all.

But his hackles raised when a scream ripped through the air.

Bryce felt his blood rush to the center of his body and then back out to his extremities again. He knew that voice. He'd never heard her scream like that, but there was a distinct note to it that he couldn't ignore. His legs instantly shot him forward, and he dodged left and right as he made his way through the thickly packed vehicles. His wolf drove him on, just as anxious to get to Dakota.

He turned to snake between two trucks, only to find that his way was blocked by a young couple making their way toward the grandstands. Bryce charged forward regardless. He didn't care what stood in his way. His mate was in trouble. Whether she wanted him to or not, he was going to do everything he could to protect her.

It wasn't that far to the tour bus, but in Bryce's mind, it took an eternity to get there. He slowed as he tried to figure out what was going on. All the lights were on inside, but the shades were pulled down. The rental car that they used for running around town was gone. Everything appeared quiet and peaceful, but he heard voices around the backside of the bus in the shadows.

"You get the hell away from my son!" Dakota said shakily as Bryce rounded the corner of the bus.

"Why can't you see that I'm just trying to show you how much I appreciate you? That's what this has been about all along."

Bryce pulled up alongside Dakota, hardly believing the scenario before his eyes. Dakota was standing with her feet apart and her fists curled. She was still in the long dress she'd been wearing when Bryce had picked Kipp up for their playdate, but she looked more than ready to fight. Across the clearing under the trees, Kipp stood holding a firefly, looking very confused. Right behind him was a man whose blonde wig had gone askew. His eyes were dark and pleading, and his jaw was set.

"Bryce!"

Hearing Dakota say his name with such relief and desperation was like music to his ears, but he'd have to focus on that later. He kept his focus on the thing that Dakota seemed most afraid of, and that was the man standing near her son. "Zane, what the hell are you doing here? I thought you were visiting your sick aunt." The blonde wig was an odd addition to the ranch hand's looks, and he'd changed his eye color, but the face was one that he'd gotten to know quite well over the last couple of months.

Dakota, never breaking her gaze from her son, reached out with one hand and gripped Bryce's elbows. Her nails sank into his skin. "I don't know who you're talking about, Bryce, but this isn't him. Nor is he Robert Barnes, as he claimed to be when I had dinner with him tonight. He's Rory Black, and he's been stalking me."

Fuck. Bryce's stomach twisted. He'd known about the stalker, and that knowledge alone had made him want to tear the guts out of anyone who threatened Dakota or made her feel uncomfortable. It was all the more damning to know that he'd been working alongside the very man himself. He could feel his wolf raging inside him. It had been simmering away for the past several days, going crazy ever since Dakota and Kipp had arrived. He hadn't bothered to let it out and work off the tension, and he wasn't sure how much longer he could hold on.

The first thing he had to do was to look out for Kipp. Bryce had no idea what Zane's intentions were, but they were obviously not good. "Kipp, you need to come over here with your mother."

The boy took a couple of steps, but he looked at Bryce quizzically. "Am I in trouble?"

"No, buddy. Just come here, please." He felt marginally better to know that Kipp wasn't within arm's reach of Zane anymore, but it wasn't as though the situation was taken care of. "You two get on the bus. I'll handle this."

"Is Robert in trouble?" the boy asked, pointing to Zane.

"What?" Bryce remembered that Dakota had also referred to him as Robert. It only made things more confusing. "Yes, he's in trouble. He's a bad man. Now I need you to go with your mom onto the bus."

"I'm not in trouble," Zane countered calmly, "and I'm not a bad man. Dakota, you and I can talk reasonably about this without your boy toy hanging around."

"I'm not talking to you, Rory. Or Zane, or whatever the hell your name is." Dakota put her hands protectively on Kipp's shoulders. "You've been following me around and driving me crazy for months, and it's time for this to come to an end."

Zane rolled his shoulders, his face a placid picture of innocence. "But don't you understand? I just have so much I want to share with you, and you won't let me in. You make yourself so hard to get close to. I wasn't trying to scare you. Once you spend some time alone with me, you'll see."

A ripple of fury shot up Bryce's spine. He was fairly certain it was accompanied by a ridge of fur, but at least his shirt and the darkness were hiding it for the moment. This asshole was just using Kipp to get to Dakota, and there was no telling what extremes he might go to. "Back off, Zane. I'm warning you!"

"Did he hurt you, Mommy?" Kipp had his feet planted firmly on the ground. His little face was tense with anger, his mouth a twisted line and his eyebrows drawn inflexibly down over his eyes. It would've been amusing if this wasn't such a serious situation.

"We can talk about that later, Kipp. Let's go. Bryce, I'll call the police."

"Don't bother." He could feel the animal inside him swelling to the surface, threatening to break free of the thin layer of humanity that kept him disguised. "I've got this."

"Me, too! I'm a wolf!"

To Bryce's horror, Kipp darted toward Zane. His little fists curled as he windmilled them through the air, and his youthful voice was made gravelly by his war cry. A slow smile spread across Zane's face, but sheer dread washed over Bryce's shoulders. His boots dug into the flattened grass below him as he shot forward after Kipp.

Whatever Bryce had thought might happen, this wasn't it. Kipp's body sprang forward, but it was no longer quite in human form. His hands and feet turned to paws covered in gray fur, and they struck the ground with natural ease as his ears morphed into their new pointed form. His back lengthened, and a tail went swinging through the air. Kipp's new teeth were tiny, but sharp as razors as he opened his mouth and prepared to attack.

A gasp of disbelief escaped Dakota.

Controlling himself was no longer an option. Bryce had held his wolf back for so long, and it practically burst out of him. He felt every individual hair of his thick coat as it shot through the surface of his skin, prickling along his shoulders. Pain tore through his skull as his bones shifted to form a muzzle. The smell he'd detected on Kipp, the one that had let him know that he had a son in the first place, was incredibly strong now. His paws thundered into the ground, and he dug in with every muscle and nail as he launched himself toward Zane. This was *his* son and *his* mate, and Zane had no right to go anywhere near them. He felt the last lengthening of his spine and gained speed.

Kipp had a head start, and he reached Zane first. His little snout tore and snapped through the air as Zane danced backward, unintimidated by the pup.

"Perhaps Dakota should've hired the two of you instead of that big old bear she keeps around," Zane said with a grin. He let out a breath and let his human side go, revealing the wolf that lived inside him.

Bryce had known that Zane was a shifter. He'd been able to tell from the moment he was hired, but he'd never imagined that the lupine creature inside him would be such a mangy mutt. His coat was thin and shaggy, and his tail was missing a few chunks of fur entirely. He had strong muscles, but his cheeks were hollow, his yellow eyes haunted.

Launching himself over Kipp's head, Bryce flew through the air and pounded into Zane. The two beasts tumbled to the ground in a tangle of paws and tails. Bryce thrashed his head to the side as he tried to get a grip on Zane's throat. He nearly did, but his enemy jerked his head out of the way as Kipp nipped his paws.

You hold him down! I'll get him! Kipp's rambunctious voice echoed in Bryce's head.

It startled him enough that he lost his position. Kipp was his son. He didn't have to be inducted into their pack in order to use the telepathic connection that some shifters shared. *Get back,* Bryce ordered as he sank his teeth into Zane's hide just in front of his tail. *Get back with your mother!*

But I want to help!

Bryce struggled. He'd only just found out he was a dad, and already he had to fight the uphill battle of parenting while in a stressful situation. He knew Kipp wanted to protect Dakota. It was the same reason Bryce was there, after all, but he couldn't risk letting the boy get hurt. *She needs you, Kipp. She's scared.*

As soon as he heard the four little paws go skittering off, Bryce dug his teeth further into Zane's flesh. The other wolf growled his irritation as he whipped around and rammed his head into Bryce's side. Bryce lost his grip with his jaws and the two of them went to the ground once again. Dust kicked up around them as they rolled, battling for the best position. Zane managed to come out on top. He thrust his nose through Bryce's paws and went for his soft underbelly.

Bryce was pinned by Zane's four paws, and the other wolf was heavier than he looked. Pain tore through him as Zane's teeth closed over his skin, but he'd be damned if he was going to let this asshole win. He flung his head to the side and clamped his teeth down on Zane's leg just above the dewclaw. He clenched his teeth with all his might, hearing the satisfying crunch of bone within flesh.

Zane yelped and leaped back, shaking his paw free of his enemy's grip. He dodged to the side as Bryce quickly sprang to his feet, and then he was off and heading for the trees. Bryce followed in hot pursuit. This fucker had threatened his mate and his son, and he wasn't going to let him get away.

Though he zipped along fairly quickly, his injured leg made it difficult for Zane to run. Bryce took the advantage he had and snapped his teeth into Zane's hind leg. He twisted his head to the side, sending Zane plummeting to the ground once again. His anger, his love, and his feral instincts drove him for one last solid push at this battle, and Bryce's teeth ripped into Zane's throat. He tore and snapped, jerking his head to the side as blood spurted over his fur. He kept going, and it wasn't until Zane had stopped moving for a minute that he realized the job was done.

Bryce panted as he stepped to the side. His muscles burned and his blood still pumped through his body at a ridiculous speed. It would be easier to recover from the battle if he remained in this form, but he knew he couldn't. Bryce forced his wolf back inside. His legs lengthened as he stood on only two of them once again, and the keen senses that came with his lupine form were muffled by this physique. His claws and paws returned to hands, and he rubbed them down his face. His shoulders sagged, knowing the hardest part was yet to come. Slowly, hoping not to scare her off, Bryce returned to the bus.

Dakota was sitting on the ground, her back leaning against a tire for support. Her hands were clutched together in front of her as she stared at her son. Fortunately, he'd already returned to the human form that Dakota had known so well. That didn't seem to put her at ease, though. Her mahogany eyes were filled with fear and uncertainty as they lifted to meet his.

"Dakota, we've got to talk."

17

"I think I'm losing my mind." Dakota's voice was a harsh whisper, and every muscle in her body ached with tension. Her little boy, her sweet baby Kipp, had transformed into an animal. As if that wasn't unbelievable enough, so had Bryce *and* her stalker, whatever his name was. "I don't understand. I—I've got to call the police. Or a mental hospital. I don't know."

"Don't do that." Bryce's hand was warm against hers as he took her cell phone from her hand. "You're not crazy, Dakota. You really did see that. It's something I've been trying to figure out how to tell you."

She quickly scooted away from him, grabbing Kipp and clinging onto him. The whole world had tilted on its side, and it had started when she'd come to Sheridan. "What did you do to him?" she demanded as she cherished the distinct humanness of Kipp against her. "What did you do to my son?"

Bryce shook his head. He was just standing there, yet she'd never been more intimidated in her life. "This isn't anything I did. It's who I am, and it's..." He trailed off as he looked down at Kipp's face.

He didn't have to finish the sentence for Dakota to understand what he meant. "You're telling me he has some sort of freak genetics?" she snapped. Tears flooded her eyes and blurred her vision. She didn't know if that was better or worse than some other answer.

"I told you I was a wolf!" Kipp volunteered.

Dakota blinked at her son. Sitting there in her lap, he truly did appear to be completely whole. There was no trace of any gray fur running down his arms, and he didn't seem to have a tail. He was smiling and happy, and if she didn't miss her mark, he actually seemed proud. "You did, baby. You definitely did." She wrapped her arms around him even tighter and rocked back and forth. There had never been a more terrifying moment in her life, but it wasn't over. She could feel that.

Bryce looked uncomfortable. He shifted his weight and rested his hands on his hips. "Uh, Kipp, your mom and I need to talk. Do you think you could go inside the bus for a moment?"

Dakota was about to argue that her son wasn't going anywhere, but just then, Frankie pulled up. She needed answers, and Kipp wasn't going to be able to give them to her like Bryce could. She did have to talk to him, whether she liked it or not. "Let's get you settled in with Grandma."

There was no time for explanations, and even though Frankie gave her some very curious looks that said she'd be getting all the details later, she took Kipp inside.

Dakota's head was swirling, and she felt as though her body was moving without her guidance when she returned to where Bryce was waiting under the trees. It was impossible not to still see what he'd turned into, even though he was standing there like any other man. She felt betrayed, conflicted, and completely bewildered. "I'll give you five minutes," she said hoarsely, "then I'm going back inside to my son."

For reasons she didn't comprehend, Bryce looked just as distraught as she did. "I'll do my best, Dakota, but this is big. You have to understand that I had to get approval to tell you, and I can't get approval for just anyone."

"No, I'll bet you can't," she said with an exhausted laugh. He still had that wild look in his eyes that had both captivated and repelled her, but at last, she knew where it came from. "And who did you have to get approval from? Nevermind. Just tell me what the hell is going on."

"Shit, this is hard," he murmured. Bryce sucked in a few deep breaths before he began. "As you saw just a few minutes ago, I'm a wolf. I'm a shifter, actually. I can change back and forth anytime I want to." He pushed the last bit of air out of his lungs. His shoulders sagged. Bryce was a tough guy, but for the first time since she'd known him, he looked pitiful.

"You're a fucking *wolf*," she whispered as she pressed her fingertips to her forehead. What he said lined up with what she saw, but it still didn't make sense. "I've heard Kipp say those exact words so many times, but I never thought it was anything but make-believe. You're telling me you can just turn into one at the drop of a hat?"

"Not just turn into one," he corrected. "It's inside me all the time, and when I'm in my wolf form, I can feel my human side. It's more like deciding which one is better for the situation, but the other one never actually goes away."

"So, what? You run around at night howling at the damn moon?" Dakota threw a hand in the air, feeling her frustration building. She'd wanted the truth, but it was too ridiculous to believe. Even though she'd just witnessed some very strange things, that didn't make any of it easy to accept.

Bryce shook his head, looking even more defeated than before. "It's not like that at all. We live pretty normal lives for the most part. We go to work and have families, and plenty of us sit around watching TV at night instead of howling at the moon. We do often live in packs, but that might be something for another day."

"We?" she squeaked. "You mean there are more?"

"Lots more. All over the country and all over the world. Actually, there are a hell of a lot more of us in Sheridan than you might ever imagine. Not all of us are wolves, though. There are shifters of all kinds of species. Bears, tigers, even a few dragons. I know it probably sounds crazy to you, but—"

"Of course, it's crazy!" Dakota raged. "This is fiction, Bryce!"

"It's not, and you have to know about it, Dakota. Your son—*our* son—is a shifter, too. He's been doing just fine as long as he had no idea, but you saw what happened. He found himself in a place where he had to defend the person he loves more than anyone else in this world, and the wolf inside him knew how to do exactly that. Now that he's had his first shift, it's all the more critical that he understands what's going on. It's not safe for people like he and I to have the whole world know who we truly are, and he's probably going to go through a phase of changing randomly, with very little control."

"So he's just going to show up for a playdate one day, get excited, and turn into an actual wolf?" Dakota was livid and desperate. She didn't know if she wanted to punch Bryce in the face or collapse into his arms.

"That's possible," he admitted. "He can learn to control it, but it's going to take time. Bryce put his hands on her arms. His grip was just gentle enough to let her know he wasn't going to hurt her, but it didn't mean she trusted him. "He needs another shifter to help him. I don't mean this as any offense to you, Dakota. You know I think you're amazing, but you're human. You have no idea what it feels like to have a wolf inside you, to hold it back when you have to, even though sometimes it hurts like hell."

"I'll figure out how to do this on my own, just like

I have for the last five years," she snapped as she tore herself from his grasp. "I can understand and even appreciate you wanting to be a part of his life, Bryce, but you can't just charge in here and claim that he absolutely needs you. I'll do it myself like I always have."

He sighed and nodded. Dakota thought he was about to give up, which filled her with both joy and disappointment. To her surprise, though, he still had more to say. "There's more you need to know, Dakota. You're not going to like it."

"As if I'm psyched about what you've already told me." Fatigue was making her eyes squint, and she felt as though she hadn't had anything to drink in weeks. She shivered despite the warm night air. Her body was completely wrung out from all the emotional stress she'd been through, not just tonight, but over the last several days. Dakota couldn't say she was surprised to be going through a bit of drama with Bryce, but she'd never envisioned it would be anything like this.

"I think you might like this even less." Bryce swallowed. "As I'm sure you can imagine, shifters aren't like regular people in a lot of ways. Probably one of the biggest is that we don't tend to fall in love with random people we happen to meet and get along with and find attractive. We find the one we're destined for. It's a completely different feeling than what we feel with anyone else. It's a bond that's created between two people's souls, and we can tell almost instantly when we find the one person we've been looking for all our lives. Sometimes that happens not just between two shifters, but between a shifter and a human. It's happened between us. We're fated to be together, Dakota. You're my mate."

She could swear there were tears in his tawny eyes, but Dakota wasn't going to feel sorry for him. "That's total bullshit and you know it."

"It's not bullshit, Dakota. It's something I've been living with ever since I met you." He dared to close the distance between them, and his finger rubbed delicately against her arm. "I admit I kind of thought it was bullshit, too, or at least I thought it was for me. It was absurd to think I would ever settle down and want to be with someone or—even stranger—that they would want to be with me. But I've been suffering with this for the last five years like a disease. I've woken up at night after having dreamt about you with such clarity, I could swear you were right there next to me. It's driven me crazy to be near you and just as crazy to be far away from you. I know that you and I are different on so many levels, but you can't tell me you haven't felt it. You can't say that you've never felt your heart reach out for me the way mine does for you."

Dakota gasped for air as hot tears burned the backs of her eyes. She did feel that, damn him. That was exactly why she'd been willing to spend time with him despite her better judgment. That stupid pull between them was the reason she'd allowed Bryce to take Kipp to the park, something that she now wished had never happened. Yes, there was a tug on her very soul when she was around him, but it couldn't be what he thought it was. "That's nothing special, Bryce. That's just lust. Sex. It isn't some sacred destiny, and I'm not going to let you talk me into believing otherwise."

"Dakota..."

"No." Her cheeks were waterfalls of tears now, and the top of her dress was getting soaked. She'd cried so many times that night, and every time she thought she'd collected herself, it just started again. She'd been spending the last few weeks wanting things to be normal, and this was so far off the mark that she couldn't even comprehend the scale anymore. "None of this changes anything between us, Bryce. I told you before that I'm going to do what's best for Kipp, and I'm still going to do that. He can be a wolf or a boy or something in between, but he's mine regardless. Now if you'll excuse me, I've got to go check on my son."

She whirled away and marched around the front of the bus, angry with herself, with Bryce, with the whole damn world.

18

"I CAN'T THANK YOU ENOUGH FOR COMING OUT HERE, Cash." Bryce watched as the deputy slammed the trunk on the bulky object wrapped in black plastic. He knew exactly what it was, but no one else would. Rory Black, or Zane, or whoever he wanted to be, would simply disappear without a trace.

"No need to thank me at all. I'm part of your pack, Bryce. I'm here for you. And there's also quite the benefit to being both a shifter and a deputy, although I can't say that clean-up duty is my favorite. You said this guy was stalking the country singer?"

"Yep." Bryce pressed his tongue to the inside of his cheek and leaned against the back of the squad car. "I knew she had a stalker, but I never imagined it would be the very guy I was bunking with back at the ranch. And to make matters worse, Dakota is my mate. Or she's supposed to be."

Cash's dark eyes lifted. "I had a feeling there was something going on there. You were distracted from the moment you stepped foot on the fairgrounds. So what's the matter? Is she mad at you for killing this guy? It sounds like you did what you had to do."

"You know that, and I know that. I'm not even sure how she feels about it, because she can't get past the idea that I'm a shifter. It's a whole new world for her, and it's one she's not interested in accepting." They were parked a short distance away from all the other vehicles, but he could easily see the glow of the camper. Dakota and Kipp were both right there, within reach. It would take only a short walk to put himself close to her once again, but he knew it wouldn't do any good. She wasn't going to see him.

The deputy let out a low whistle. "That's rough. Did you talk to Shaw?"

"Oh, yeah. He's the one who gave me permission to tell her in the first place. I don't know if she would've taken it well regardless, and I pretty much figured she wouldn't, but I don't think it helped that she got her first introduction to shifters by seeing both me and our son turn into wolves right in front of her eyes. You know how humans are. They're too focused on the fact that you ought to belong in a horror movie."

"That's true enough," Cash laughed. "I think about that sometimes when I pull over a tourist. If they had any idea just how many of us were up here, they'd probably hit the highway and never come back. Hey, you said you were working with this guy?" He tapped the lid of the trunk.

"Yep. Colton and Willa's latest hire. I don't think they're going to be pleased. We all knew he was a little quiet and strange, but we didn't think he was like that." Bryce scratched his forehead. Being short a hand on the ranch was going to present a whole new problem that would need to be taken care of, but he had enough of his own. He'd just do his job and let Colton and Willa deal with it. They were more than capable.

"I take it he was staying at the bunkhouse you guys built? I'd like to come take a look at the place if you don't think Colton would mind. If this guy was a stalker, then there's probably some evidence there I need to see."

"Sure thing. I'll call them up, and then I'll meet you out there." He dialed his boss as he headed back to his truck. Colton, like any rancher who got up with the sun, had been in bed for quite some time.

He was easy to rouse, though. Ranchers had to be, just in case an animal was sick or some other emergency happened. Willa jumped on the other line, and once they'd heard the story, they gave their full permission for Cash to do whatever he needed to.

"Both you and Caleb can come stay in the main house with us until we get this figured out," Willa said, her voice sympathetic over the phone. "There's plenty of room."

"Sure." He hung up, not feeling particularly excited about having a slumber party. Not that he wanted to be in the bunkhouse, either. Maybe he'd just go camp somewhere and be alone.

Cash pulled in the driveway behind him, down the hill, and around to the bunkhouse. Colton was waiting for them out front, the keys in his hand.

"Sorry to get you up at this hour," Cash said as he got out.

Colton rubbed a hand over his face, erasing the last bit of sleep. "Don't be sorry at all. Things need to be done, and that doesn't always mean we can stick to a schedule." He led the way inside.

"Pretty nice place," Cash said as they stepped into the main living area. "Which room was Zane's?"

"Right over here." Colton tried the doorknob, but it was locked. He flicked through the keys he'd brought with him, got it open, and stepped aside so that Cash could go in first.

"Holy shit." Cash let out a low whistle. "Have any of you guys seen this?"

Though he wasn't sure he wanted to, Bryce poked his head in the door. His heart clenched when he saw the numerous photos that had been plastered to the walls. Some of them were the same ones he'd seen online when he'd been curious about Dakota's life. There were magazine clippings from her concerts and her interviews. Computer printouts of her red-carpet outfits were tacked all along the wall above Zane's desk. Posters, concert tickets, signed albums, and t-shirts were interspersed with these.

"You can come in, just don't touch anything," Cash advised.

Bryce's wolf was going crazy all over again. To know that someone was this obsessed with *his* mate was disturbing, to say the least. He wished Zane would come back to life just so he could kill him all over again. "This sick fucker."

"You never saw any of this?" Cash asked as he began taking photos.

"He was pretty private. Well, all of us were except for Caleb. We just kind of stayed out of each other's rooms, and Zane didn't even hang out with us in the living area." Bryce noticed the layout of the room and the fact that none of the memorabilia had been placed where someone would see it if Zane was going in or out of the room. It had all been put up on the opposite side, giving the impression that everything was perfectly normal if someone happened to glance in.

"Check this out." Colton bent down to peer into a small shadow box that sat on the dresser. "It just looks like a big splinter of wood, but he's got it labeled. It's a piece of the stage from one of her shows further out west."

"And then there's this." Cash had opened the closet doors to reveal a series of Styrofoam heads, each bearing wigs of different colors and lengths. "He was a well-organized stalker, that's for sure. There are drawers in here with colored contacts, prosthetic noses, glasses, and several fake IDs."

"You all right?" Colton was studying Bryce closely. "You look a little pale."

"I ought to be. I was living and working right alongside the guy, and I never had a clue. He was weird and reserved, but so am I. Holy hell." He'd just spun in a slow circle to take in the full extent of their find, and he'd noticed something on the back of the bedroom door. Pushing it closed with the toe of his boot revealed a bulletin board with a map of the United States and several other pieces of paper tacked around it.

Cash stepped up behind him. "Color-coded pins for each of her tours, a different one for each year. He must've planned out exactly where she'd be and set himself up here on the ranch so that he'd already be established in Sheridan before she ever got here."

"The charity auction gave him the perfect excuse to find some alone time with her, even though I don't think that was organized until much more recently. Zane must've been thrilled when he found out, the bastard. And then Dakota set herself up perfectly by not letting her bodyguard supervise the dinner. Damn it!" Bryce slammed his fist into the doorframe, sending a shower of tiny splinters down onto the floor. "Sorry."

"I don't think any of us blame you for being angry," Colton said softly. "Hell, I was the one dumb enough to hire him. I should've sensed something in him."

"No, don't start playing the blame game," Cash advised. "I may not have been with the sheriff's department for all that long, but I've already learned that sometimes things just happen to people. We can't always control it or predict it, so don't go around thinking it's all your fault."

Bryce wasn't sure he could just dismiss himself of any fault in this. Dakota was his mate. She was the one person he was absolutely connected to in the universe, and he should've known. Not that she gave a shit about it, but he did.

"I think I've got all the photos I need for now. If you could do me a favor and keep this room locked up in case there's anything further that we need, I'd appreciate it."

Colton shook the deputy's hand. "You know you've got it. Bryce, come on up to the house. Willa has been fussing over getting the guest rooms ready ever since we found out about this, and the next thing I know, she'll be baking cookies."

"Yeah. I'll be there in a bit. I just need a second."

Colton headed up to the house, and Cash and Bryce headed back toward their vehicles.

"So what happens now? With you and Dakota? Are you just going to let her go?"

"I don't really see that I have a choice," Bryce replied bitterly. "I've thought a million times about trying again, but she's beyond angry with me. She thought I'd be a bad influence on Kipp even before she knew the truth, and I've only made it worse by telling her."

Cash turned on his cell screen. His wallpaper was set to a photo of his little girl, Addy. "I can't imagine that, man. And what about his shifting? I know Addy is already letting out her inner dragon, and she's pretty uncontrollable. I don't mean to make you feel any worse about what you've got going on, but how is a human going to handle that?"

Bryce leaned on the fence. "Her bodyguard is a shifter," he grumbled.

"No shit. Does she know?" Something came through on Cash's radio, and he quickly replied.

"Nope, and I'm not going to tell her. That's Tyler's business, and I have a good feeling it's all going to come out pretty soon. He knows about me, and he knows about Kipp. He cares a lot about them, and he's already told me he'd planned on being there for Kipp once his wolf came out. There's no point in driving away the one shifter Kipp is pretty much guaranteed to have in his life, even if he isn't blood. I can take some small amount of consolation from knowing Tyler will be there for him, but I can't say I'm happy about any of this." He looked out over the fields and pastures illuminated by moonlight. Bryce had found a great life there on the Ward Ranch. His childhood had been beyond rough, and that'd made the transition into the adult world just as difficult. He'd been pretty lost for a long time, and it wasn't until he'd come there and found a steady place with people who cared about him that he'd become more than just a wanderer.

Now, he felt himself craving something even more stable than what he already had. A good job working for good people was fantastic, but he was still just a bachelor living in a bunkhouse. He wanted a good, solid woman at his side. He wanted to share his life with Kipp and hopefully let the boy learn from his own mistakes without having to make them himself.

Would things be any different if he were a human? If he could just give up his wolf and be like anyone else? He wasn't sure, but the damn beast didn't exactly make things easier.

"You should talk to her," Cash said quietly, interrupting his brooding.

Bryce snorted. "You sound just like Shaw."

"There's a lot we could all learn from the man," the deputy admitted. "He basically told me to throw myself at Shiloh's feet and let her decide my fate. It sounded extreme, but he was right. It's not like any of us—men or women—can decide alone what's going to happen with our relationships. It has to be both of us. Shiloh and I weren't communicating about how we truly felt, and it was only hurting us. It wasn't until we quit being so damn stubborn that we figured out we were a lot more aligned in our thoughts than we realized."

"But I *have* talked to her," Bryce reasoned. He gripped the top board of the fence and stretched backward, but it didn't do anything to take the tension out of his shoulders. His muscles had been bound into knots ever since he'd shifted. He'd held his wolf inside for far too long, and now he was paying the price. "She doesn't want to hear any of it. She thinks it's all just crazy bullshit. Hell, she didn't come right out and say it, but I get the idea she thinks I'm just making all this up to manipulate her into being with me."

"You've talked to her *once,*" Cash corrected, "and that was right after she'd first found out that shifters even existed. It all feels normal for us, but it's got be really hard for someone who's always thought people were just people. Ask Willa about it. I'm sure she'd be happy to give you some advice."

"Yeah, maybe." Bryce liked Willa, and he had no doubt she'd be willing to sit and chat with him about anything. She was certainly their resident expert when it came to explaining these things to humans. "The thing is, I don't have a lot of time. Her concert is tomorrow, and then she's picking up and leaving town. She'll head off on the rest of her tour, and I'd be willing to bet I'll never see her again. If she has any choice in the matter, she'll probably never come back to Sheridan."

Cash slapped the fence. "Then that's exactly why you need to find some way to talk to her. Maybe that bodyguard can help you."

"I don't know." Bryce felt completely defeated. Hell, he was standing there pouring his heart out in the wee hours of the morning to Cash. He liked the guy, but that just wasn't something he did. He kept his pain and fear buried deep where it belonged, and up until that week, he hadn't had any intentions of changing that. Dakota and Kipp, however, had changed everything.

"Give it a shot. Then at least you'll know you tried. If she still won't have anything to do with you, then no one can fault you or claim that you didn't do your best, especially you." Cash clapped him on the shoulder. "I'd better get the rest of this evidence over to the department so Levi can look at it in the morning. This guy might be dead now, but he's still going to want to know about it. Let me know if there's anything I can do for you."

"Thanks, Cash." Bryce stood there long after the deputy had left. If he looked out over the rolling hills, it was easy to pretend that he was the only man in the world. He sure as hell felt like it.

19

THINGS HAD BEEN QUIET ON THE TOUR BUS SINCE THE night before. Kipp had slept like a log while Dakota stayed up late talking to her mother and Tyler. Frankie had listened with confusion and disbelief, but once Tyler confirmed that he'd heard of things like this before, she became far more accepting.

Dakota wished that she could accept it. She'd been wrestling with it ever since the previous evening. She'd showered thoroughly, wishing she could wash it all away and forget that any of this had ever happened. She'd tried to sleep, but she'd only managed to doze a little between restlessly thrashing around. The image of her son transforming from a boy to a wolf simply refused to leave her mind. So did Bryce.

"Hey, honey." A gentle knock sounded on her bedroom door, and it slid to the side to reveal Frankie. "I just thought I'd check in on you and see if you're ready for the show."

"Not really." Dakota leaned over her guitar, feeling the comforting familiarity of the hollow body against her. She flicked a finger against the crumpled papers that held the lyrics and notes she'd been working on. "I finished my song, but that's about it."

"Can I hear it?" Frankie was giving her that look again. It was the same one she'd used when Dakota was in eighth grade and had botched her solo in the chorus concert, and it was also the same look she'd worn when Dakota had told her she was pregnant. It was a look that said everything would be okay, and her mother was going to do everything in her power to make sure Dakota knew that.

She appreciated it, but Dakota couldn't be cajoled into believing that everything was fine simply because her mother wanted it to be. "No, not right now. I'm not sure I'm ready for it."

Frankie glanced at the words on the pages, but she didn't read them outright. "Are you going to perform it tonight?"

"No way." Dakota stuffed the sheets in her guitar

case, where she always put the music she was working on to make sure she had it handy when she was feeling creative. "I just want to get this performance over with and put it all behind me."

"Dakota." Frankie put her hand on her daughter's knee. "We need to talk."

"We *have* talked. I need to get ready."

Her mother gave her a completely different look this time, the one that said she'd better listen. "I know perfectly well just how fast you can get yourself ready for an appearance when you want to, and for all I care, you can get dressed while I'm right here in the room with you. But we can't just pretend none of this happened. We're going to need to get this figured out."

"I know, and we will," Dakota said dismissively. She ran a cloth over the flame maple top of her guitar and put it in the case. "But it's not like I can just analyze this problem and come up with a solution in a matter of minutes, or even a few days. I never knew this about my son, and it's going to change all of our lives. I don't have a clue how I'm going to handle it, or if I even can while we're on the road. I might have to just cancel the rest of my tour and forget about doing any of this ever again." She shook her head. That would've actually sounded great not too long ago when she'd been fed up with cameras in her face, stalkers, and constant scrutiny from the media. Now, it just seemed incredibly unfair that she might have to give up everything she'd worked so hard for because of this.

"I don't think you'll have to go to any extremes. We'll work it out, just like everything else," Frankie soothed. "You didn't give your career up when you got pregnant, and you only took a small amount of time when Kipp was born. You were right back in the studio after that, and if you didn't have to give up your career due to having a son, then I don't think you have to just because he's a little different."

"Yeah. Maybe not." Dakota knew she was just feeling sorry for herself, but she couldn't help it. She opened the closet and looked at her options. Nothing looked particularly exciting, and she was concerned that this was going to end up being a horrible show. Her first Sheridan show had been the one that had launched her into stardom, but with the mood she was in, this show might send her to the bottom of the charts. She finally selected a denim shirt and a white skirt with a wide brown belt. It looked cute, but it was also incredibly comfortable. If Dakota could get away with wearing her pajamas onstage, then she would.

Frankie bit her lower lip. "I think there's more than just the problem with Kipp."

Dakota buttoned the shirt and looked at her mother over her shoulder. "What do you mean?"

"Bryce."

"Ha!" Dakota was too tired to laugh for real, but the thought of doing anything about Bryce was just laughable. "Mom, he's a nut. I told you all that crap he piled on about us being destined to be together. It's ridiculous. I've already let him invade my life far too much, and it's time for it to stop."

Frankie wasn't the kind of woman to give up so easily. "But you feel quite a bit for him." It wasn't a question.

Dakota shoved the tails of her shirt into her skirt and whipped the belt around her waist. She sucked in a breath, prepared to tell her mom just exactly how much she hated Bryce. But there were no words that supported that stance that would come to her lips. "I'm mad at him," she said instead. "He didn't tell me the truth."

"And neither did you," Frankie pointed out. "He's been missing out on his son's life all this time. I can understand why you felt you were making the right decision, but I can also see how he probably felt the same way, given the circumstances. You were both keeping secrets to protect yourselves. Now that it's all out in the open, I think it's time you step back and think about how you really feel."

"I don't..." Dakota trailed off as a sob choked her throat. "Shit." She crumpled onto the bed as tears streamed down her face.

"It's all right, baby." Frankie pulled her head over into her lap and stroked her hair. She moved slightly as she reached over to grab a tissue from the dresser and handed it to Dakota. "It's not always easy to think about how we really feel. I think society teaches us that a lot of that has to be stuffed down so that we can work and be successful and not let anyone else know how weak we are inside. But there's so much more to life than that, honey."

"I just don't know what to do, Mom. When he told me that, I was so angry that I didn't want to hear it. I didn't think he could possibly be right. But I can't stop thinking about him. I even wrote that whole damn song about him. How can someone I barely know become such a huge part of my life?" Her makeup was completely ruined now, and she'd probably be late for the show, but she didn't care.

Frankie laughed. "We're all under the impression that we get to choose who we're with, but it doesn't really work that way. Not even for us humans. When I met your father, I knew he was exactly the kind of person my parents wouldn't want me to be with. Even I thought he wasn't a good fit, but I just couldn't help myself. It was a beautiful marriage, and I have no doubts that if he were still alive, we'd be together today. You notice I haven't even bothered trying to date again. I just don't see the point."

"I never realized." Dakota hadn't given much thought to her mother's love life at all, in fact. It made Bryce's revelation make a little more sense. She sat up and wiped her face. "Love sucks."

"You'll get no arguments from me. We don't leave until tomorrow morning, so you have a little time to think about it. Maybe you could at least do yourself the favor of talking to him and go from there."

"We'll see. I'd better go wash my face and start over." Dakota headed into the bathroom to remove the last of her ruined makeup and reapply for the concert.

The next couple of hours went by swiftly. Tyler took her to the grandstands for a few sound checks before they let the audience in. She could hear them even as they waited outside the gate, their screams of excitement carrying through the air. They wanted her. They'd come from all over the surrounding area to see her, and they lined up at the merchandise booths. When the time came, they streamed into the grandstands like water. They filled up every available seat, and the fairgrounds had even put together floor seating right down in front of the stage. Before long, hardly anything was visible except bodies and faces, all lined up to see her show. Her fans deserved a good performance, and Dakota knew she'd have to put her emotional struggles aside to do her job. She'd done it before, and even though this time it seemed that weight of her mind was too heavy to put down, she could do it again.

Tyler was at her elbow, looking carefully out into the audience. "You ready?"

Dakota looked up at her bodyguard, finding comfort in his presence. "I think so. Or at least, I'm as ready as I can be. What are you looking for? My stalker has already been taken care of, so it's not like we need to worry about him anymore."

His face was calm as he continued to scan the audience. "I'm just doing my job."

There was something in his voice that sounded a little too sad, and Dakota had to wonder if Tyler had taken some of his free time to start his own little romance while they were there in Sheridan. How funny would it be if he were staring out over the audience because he was hoping a special lady had shown up?

A woman Dakota had briefly met earlier from the local radio station came by with a grin on her face. "They're all worked up and ready to go. All set?"

Dakota simply gave her a nod

The radio announcer headed out to center stage and took the mic. The audience went wild with cheers of anticipation before she even said anything, and she waited patiently for the noise to die down. "Thank you, Sheridan! I know we've kept you waiting long enough, but I just wanted to thank all the people who made this happen."

Dakota closed her eyes. She touched the frets and strings on her guitar, her fingers finding all the right places as though they could see. There was a place deep inside her where only the music lived, and she desperately needed to tap into it right now. She let go of the rest of the world. There was nothing she could do about it right now.

"Here she is, the woman you've all been waiting for and my favorite artist, Dakota Jones!"

She opened her eyes. Her kilowatt smile erupted

on her face as she stepped forward and nodded to the radio announcer. She wasn't Dakota Jones, mother, daughter, and woman who had no idea what she was going to do about the wolves in the world. She was simply Dakota Jones, country superstar. "Hello, Sheridan! You're a beautiful crowd! Let's get things started with something a little upbeat."

The drums and bass started up. The lights changed colors and spun. Dakota ran through her set just as she did in any other large venue. It was a run that mixed cheerful party songs with ballads, hit songs with B-sides, both new and old. She allowed herself to enjoy how automatic it was at this phase in the game. These songs were so much a part of her that she never had to think about what the next lyric was or which chord she should be playing. They were as natural as breathing, and it was exactly what she needed. Dakota had been dreading this concert because of everything Sheridan had meant to her before, but she'd forgotten that the performance itself was still just as pure, raw, and wonderful of a ride as it would be anywhere else she went.

Far too soon, the set was finished. The drummer and bassist played their final outros as she strummed the last chords and put her hand up in the air to wave. "Thank you so much, Sheridan! You've been an amazing crowd!"

The autopilot she'd been on shut off right then. There was no denying the reality of the world any longer as she stepped back from the mic, even with a screaming audience still standing in front of her. Dakota's fingers closed around the neck of the guitar again, automatically forming the chords of the song she'd been working so hard on over the past day.

She pressed her tongue against her teeth, trying to decide. She hadn't rehearsed this in front of an audience at all. It was finished, but barely. It wasn't the kind of thing she would normally just introduce in a packed crowd without first having played it for her producer, her manager, and her mother, people she trusted to tell her if it needed more work or if it just wasn't going to fly.

But Dakota knew she needed to get this out, and she couldn't think of a better place to do it than right there. "If y'all don't mind, I'd like to debut a new song for you."

They didn't mind at all if their thunderous screams had anything to do with it.

"Thank you," she said with a little laugh, flattered that they were all so supportive. It touched her, and she felt that familiar burning at the backs of her eyes. "This is a song I just wrote. I think it's pretty relevant, considering that even though I'd played at many other places, the Sheridan Rodeo was where I truly got my start. Just bear with me. It's a very personal song, and I might mess up a little."

More screams. "We love you, Dakota!"

"I love you, too." She covered the mic and turned to her band members. "Don't worry, guys. This one's just me."

Her notes were in her guitar case, but Dakota knew she didn't need them. She centered herself again as she began playing, losing herself in the music. "This is where it all started, just you and I," she began.

The audience went crazy. Dakota knew each person would take this song and make it personal to them, but she absolutely knew what it meant to her. It was all about Bryce. She'd tried to deny her feelings for him because it was easier. She already shared her life with the whole country, but sharing all the little things with a partner was new territory.

"It's not easy for me to say how much I love you. It's the sort of thing I never thought I was meant to do." She closed her eyes and tipped her head back, feeling her emotions well up and bubble over. Tears like hot lava streamed down her face. Dakota knew what she would have to do. She'd have to find Bryce and tell him what an idiot she'd been. He couldn't help who he was inside. It wasn't the sort of thing that was easy for her to understand, but she could sure try a lot harder than she had. Kipp needed his father, and—as crazy as it seemed—she needed her mate. She just hoped that she'd be able to find him again.

She hit the final chorus. "I have so many places and things to do, but the world keeps bringing me right back home to you." Her fingers plucked out the last few notes, a reverberating sadness that she felt in her heart. Slowly, she opened her eyes. The clamor from the grandstands and the floor was deafening, and it crashed down on her and pulled even more tears from the depths of her soul.

"Thank you," she choked out as she skimmed the crowd. She was just about to run back to the tour bus when she realized who was in the audience. Bryce was right there in the front row, looking up at her. Dakota moved to him and fell to her knees in front of him. "What are you doing here?"

"I had to see you one last time." Those dark amber eyes were still untamed, but Dakota didn't see them the same way anymore.

"No. Not the last time," she said, reaching out to

touch his cheek. His skin electrified her, and she didn't understand how she'd been such a fool. "Not if I have anything to say about it." She kissed him soundly, focusing only on the way her lips felt against his instead of the screaming audience all around them.

20

BRYCE FROWNED AT HIS PHONE SCREEN. HE MARKED one listing so he could remember to check it out in more detail later and kept scrolling. There were a lot of possibilities and things he needed to think about.

"Still have your nose in the classifieds?"

He put down the phone to find Willa hovering over him, her hands on her hips. "I am."

She jabbed a finger in the air toward the clock hanging over the fireplace. "You're going to be late."

"Shit. I completely lost track of time." Bryce bounced up off the couch and headed into the guest room. He'd already packed pretty much everything he needed, and he didn't consider himself to be particularly high-maintenance. He'd never taken a trip like this, though, and that made it hard to be sure he wasn't missing anything.

"Do you need any help?" Willa had followed him and was still hovering in the doorway.

He skimmed a hand over his head. His stomach dipped, just as it did every time he thought about what he was about to do. "I didn't get the last few things out of the bunkhouse. I've just got to do that."

"Don't worry about it. We'll take care of it, and we'll keep all your extra things for you until you come back." Willa put a hand on his arm and smiled. "We're all really happy for you, Bryce."

Bryce gave her a look. "Don't go getting all mushy on me now. You know I don't like it."

"Of course, I do. That's exactly why I have to do it before you leave. You're like the brother I never had, and I have to give you a bit of a hard time, don't I?"

Damn, he was going to miss her. He was going to miss this whole place, but not enough to make him change his mind. He gave her a brief hug and felt her body stiffen in surprise before she hugged him back. "Yeah, I guess you do."

Grabbing his suitcase, Bryce headed out to the barn to check in with Colton. The rancher shook his hand. "It's been great to have you here, man. There will always be work waiting here for you if you need it."

"Thank you. You guys have been like family to me, you know. It's good to know I can always come home again." Bryce clapped him on the arm and headed into town before he got too emotional.

The bus was right there waiting for him, having delayed its departure for this new turn of events. Bryce looked at the long, sleek vehicle as it pulled up. It was hard to imagine that this would be his home for the next several months. He knew he could manage when it came to sharing a small space with other people and the constantly changing scenery, at least. He just hoped he could handle it in other ways.

Right on cue, Dakota descended the bus steps as he got out of his truck. She'd lightly curled her hair, and it floated down around her shoulders as she walked up to him. "Hey. Did you get everything?"

Bryce hauled his suitcase out of the truck. "As long as it isn't too much."

"Not at all. Is someone coming by to pick up your vehicle?"

"I left the spare keys back at the ranch with Caleb. I'm going to let him drive it and keep it up while I'm gone."

She stepped closer and laid her hand on his

chest. When she looked up at him, there was so much love and worry in her eyes. "Are you sure this is what you want?"

There was a lot of uncertainty about what they were about to do, but he didn't have any doubt about this. Dakota was his mate, and she was finally willing to let him into her life. They both had a lot of work to do if they were going to make this work, but he was up for it. He'd never be able to live with himself if he didn't try. "Definitely."

"Me, too." She kissed him, taking her time and pressing her fingertips into his strong chest. "I think we've got everything packed up and ready to go. That just leaves one thing to do if you're ready."

His throat tightened. Bryce was nervous as hell, but he was also really looking forward to this. "I'm ready."

"I think he is, too." Dakota went back to the bus for a moment and came back with Kipp. "Sweetie, come sit over here under the trees with us. There's something Bryce and I would like to talk to you about."

Kipp, dressed in a plaid shirt, jeans, and a giant souvenir belt buckle, looked from one to the other. "Am I in trouble? I didn't mean to get the couch hairy."

"Oh, honey. You're not in trouble at all." Dakota gave an embarrassed look to Bryce. "He grew a bit of fur while we were curled up watching a movie last night."

"These things happen," Bryce reasoned. He did his best to stay calm on the outside, but his heart was soaring. This was his son, and he was truly coming into his own. He'd shifted the first time by accident, and that wasn't unusual. There would be many more times when he'd experience his sharper set of teeth suddenly come through when he got angry or find that he was wagging his tail when he was happy. Bryce was actually going to get the chance to help him through all of that.

Dakota knelt next to her son. "Kipp, you like Bryce, right?"

"Yeah! He's a wolf! Like me! Grrr!"

Without really thinking about it, Bryce held out his hand to get a high-five and was rewarded with the slap of Kipp's tiny palm against his.

"That's right." Dakota's face twitched a little. Bryce knew she was still trying to get used to this idea. "How would you feel if Bryce came along on the rest of the tour with us?"

Kipp's eyes opened wide. "Really? You're going to come with us?" he shouted.

"If you don't mind," Bryce replied.

Dakota rubbed her lips together. "Um, you know why you and Bryce are so much alike? Well, Bryce is your father. He's your daddy. How does that make you feel?"

Kipp turned his astonished eyes up to Bryce's, his lower lip going slack as he contemplated the news.

Bryce hadn't thought he was ready to be a father. Now that he was standing there, waiting to see what Kipp had to say about it, he couldn't wait to step into the role. The two of them shared a genetic link regardless of how the boy felt about it, but Bryce found himself tensing up as he waited to hear Kipp's response. He wanted Kipp to like him. He wanted so badly to make up for everything he didn't have as a child himself. It wouldn't be easy, and he knew that, but he would go to the end of the world and back for this kid. He hadn't been a good mate or father so far, but he could be. He felt his wolf reaching out to connect with the beast inside this little boy.

"You're my daddy?" Kipp asked.

"I am." Bryce swallowed as he knelt. "You okay with that?"

Kipp had been completely stunned, but now his eyes went wild with excitement as he threw his arms around Bryce's shoulders. "Yeah!"

Bryce hugged him back and pressed his cheek against him. He was holding the entire world in his hands. Tears threatened once again as he realized this must've been exactly what Dakota had gone through in all the years she'd been raising him. Bryce couldn't blame her one bit for trying to do everything possible to keep him safe, even if that meant avoiding the uncertainty of letting Bryce into his life. "I love you, buddy."

"Love you, too, Daddy!" Kipp replied as he pulled back. "I gotta go tell Grandma!"

Dakota shook her head with amusement as she watched her son get back on the bus. "She already knows, of course, but I'm not going to spoil it for him."

"She's not upset about it, is she?" Bryce kicked himself on the inside for suddenly caring so damn much about what everyone else thought. He'd never cared before.

"Nope. You're family." Dakota wove her fingers between his as the bus's engine rumbled to life. "And I think it might actually work out quite well for her. There are going to be some things that only you can teach Kipp, and that means she has more time for shopping and spa days."

They boarded the bus for the last time. Tyler was

in the driver's seat, checking the gauges and waiting for everyone to settle in. He reached out to shake Bryce's hand as he came up the steps behind Dakota. "Good to have you on board. Guess I'll have to start teaching you how to do my job."

"What do you mean?" Many details still needed to be discussed about their future, but the fate of Tyler's position hadn't come up. "I can't imagine Dakota would let you go."

Tyler tweaked an eyebrow and gave the slightest smile. "We'll see about that."

A few minutes later, the bus glided forward and away from the fairgrounds. Bryce sat near the window at the dinette, watching as Sheridan slipped by and then gave way to fields and highway. It was strange to think that he was leaving, but if everything went the way he planned, he'd be coming back soon enough.

"I'm heading into the back to work on some music. I'll let you two have some time together." Dakota kissed Bryce on the head and ruffled Kipp's hair. She gestured with her head at her mother, and the two of them went to the far end of the bus.

Bryce leaned forward, watching as Kipp scribbled in a coloring book. "You're the expert when it comes to being on tour. Got any advice for me?"

The boy lifted a shoulder as he selected a different crayon. "Mommy says it's an adventure and just to have fun."

Bryce nodded, thinking that could apply not just to their trip, but to the entire escapade of parenthood that still lay before him. "Seems like good advice to me."

21

THE LEAVES WERE CHANGING WHEN THEY ROLLED BACK into Sheridan three months later. Dakota felt the familiar zip of energy racing through her body that she often got that time of year. There was something about the change in seasons that always inspired her creativity, and she'd already written two songs just that week. By the time she got into the studio, her producer would have a tough time figuring out how many tracks to put on the next album.

For the moment, though, she was already working out the details of her next tour.

"Are you sure?" Ray asked over the phone, sounding a bit baffled.

"Of course, I'm sure."

He let out a sound of exasperation. "I think you're going to end up losing a lot of ticket sales, which means the tour might not turn out to be worth the cost."

Dakota smiled to herself. She knew that would be part of his argument when she took the idea to him, but she didn't care. "It might not be the biggest money-maker, but that's not the point. We're talking about smaller venues, yes, but that means we'll be bringing the show to people who otherwise might not be able to make it into the bigger cities to see it."

It was easy to envision him sitting in his office, scratching his balding head as he tried to figure this out. "I don't know..."

"Are you saying you won't do what I ask?" Dakota challenged.

"Well, I just...It's my job to do what's best for your career, Dakota, and I worry that this might not be the right choice."

"Ray, this is what I'm doing. Whether it's with or without you is up to you," she replied pointedly.

"Fine, fine. Let's finalize a few other details, then."

She got off the phone a few minutes later, just as they pulled up next to a hotel.

"You look pleased with yourself," Bryce noted as she came out of the bedroom. "Did you get it all set?"

"I sure did. He was hesitant at first, but even Ray understands how much commission he'd lose if he forced me to use someone different. He's getting on it right now, so it's all official. The 'Not My First Rodeo' Tour will be stopping at rodeos all over the country next summer. No stadiums, no football arenas. Just simple, outdoor stages where I can really get to know the people who've made my career what it is."

"Congratulations." Bryce pulled her forward by the hips and kissed her. He kept her close as he looked into her eyes. "Now, I need you to come with me. I have a surprise for you."

"But we've got to get the bus unloaded so Tyler can take it in for repairs. I can't just leave that to everyone else," Dakota argued as they moved toward the front of the bus.

"Honey, we've been on this bus for three months. I wouldn't trade the experience for the world, but right now, I need my boots on the ground. Just trust me on this one."

Tyler jerked his head toward the door. "You'd better get going before your new bodyguard gets upset. You're not going to find a better replacement. We'll be here when you get back."

"Can I go, too?" Kipp asked. He was dressed as a cowboy once again, something he'd taken a particular liking to even after finding out that he really was a wolf inside. The boy had fully embraced that part of himself, but when he was concentrating on being a human, he was more interested in bull riding and roping. Bryce had assured Dakota that every boy—even shifter boys—went through different phases and interests.

"No, buddy. This is a surprise for Mommy, but you'll get to see it soon enough. I promise." Bryce tweaked the front of Kipp's hat down with his finger, causing an eruption of giggles.

"Okay, Daddy. Grandma, let's go explore the hotel! I wonder if they have those little soaps!" Kipp grabbed Frankie's hand and dragged her off the bus.

"It sounds like I'm the only one surprised by whatever this surprise is," Dakota noted. She smelled the cold, clean air that signified winter would be coming soon.

Bryce grinned. "I might've discussed things with them a little just to make sure I got it right. I think I did. Ah, here it is. Caleb left my truck for us."

They climbed into the cab. Dakota expected him to stop at a store or something, but he just kept going. They headed out of town and down long, winding roads. The sky was big and beautiful over them, with the sun blazing down on fields that were beginning to turn from deep green to pale brown. "Where are we going?"

"Hang on. We're almost there." Bryce slowed down and turned onto a narrow driveway surrounded by farm fields on either side. The truck bounced over a few washouts and potholes as they headed further off the main track until he finally pulled up in front of an old white farmhouse.

Dakota leaned forward to examine the two-story home with its stone fireplace and covered front porch. "This is cute. Who lives here?"

"We do." Bryce handed her a set of keys.

"What?" Dakota's jaw went slack as she stared down at the keys in her palm and then up at the house. Of all the things she'd imagined he might be trying to surprise her with, this hadn't been it. "What?" she repeated.

Bryce laughed as he got out and headed around the side of the house. "Come on. I'll show you."

Dakota hopped out and followed him, still caught up in disbelief. "You bought us a house?"

"I sure did. Unlock the front door!"

With shaking fingers, she did as he asked. It took

a second, but she opened it up to find hardwood floors, ancient wallpaper, and a tall set of stairs that led up to the second level. Dakota moved through the place in sheer awe. "It's so old," she said as she ran a hand down the farm table that still sat in the kitchen. "And it needs a ton of work. I love it!"

"I was hoping you would. You see, you already talked about finding a way to balance things out a little better for Kipp. We can stay here in the winter months while you're writing and planning out your future tours. Kipp can go to school right here in Sheridan. I'll spend my time fixing up the house and helping out at the Ward Ranch, which isn't far from here. There's an in-law's cabin out by the garage, so Frankie can stay with us and still have her own space. And look out the back door. There's a grove back there with just enough room for us to put up a writing shed for when you need to get away and work on your music."

"I'm blown away," Dakota whispered. It was exactly what she would've picked out herself, something that had modern conveniences paired with the warmth and history of an older home. It was their own private space where they could pretend to be perfectly normal when not on tour.

"You haven't even seen the best part." Bryce, more excited than she'd probably ever seen him, grabbed her hand and led her up the stairs. He turned and raced down to the end of the hallway, where he stopped and scooped her up into his arms. "I should've done this downstairs, but this should be just as good."

Dakota laughed as he pushed the door open with his boot to reveal the master bedroom. It was huge, with wide windows that looked out over the gorgeous Wyoming landscape and reminded her of just how alone they were in the world. There was a separate fireplace there, and someone had already remodeled the old house at some point to include an en suite bathroom with a large tub.

"I see you've already started decorating," Dakota said, gesturing toward the massive bed in the middle of the room.

He fell onto the mattress with her and laughed as he began kissing her neck. "I had to make a few arrangements. I wanted to be able to demonstrate exactly what we can do while we're living here eight or nine months out of the year."

Dakota looked up at the ceiling above them. It hadn't been easy to find time alone while they'd been on the road. Oh, they'd made do, but this was going to be so much better. She moved her hands over Bryce's muscular shoulders as he kissed his way down the front of her neck and into the space exposed by the undone buttons on her shirt. His fingers slowly unfastened the rest, his hands gliding under the fabric to ripple down her ribs.

She shivered in the cool air of the home, thrilled to know that they truly were alone. Yes, she'd be spending plenty of time working on her songs, and Bryce would have a lot to keep himself occupied, but she had no doubt that they'd return there together night after night to talk, snuggle, and make love. Dakota's body tingled under his kisses as she understood the depth of the gift he'd given her.

Bryce pushed himself backward and off the bed, standing at the foot of it as he pulled her jeans from her hips and flung them aside. They hit the window and fell to the floor with a thump. He grabbed her by the hips and pulled her forward, his caramel eyes meeting hers for a moment before he kissed her just below her navel. His attention swiftly moved downward, and Dakota was ready for him when his heated lips closed on her. She gasped, writhing under the quick flicks of his tongue that teased and provoked her. Her body convulsed and shuddered, and combined with the excitement of the house, it was almost too much to handle. Dakota pushed backward, but Bryce's hands closed around her hips and he yanked her back down toward him with a growl. She gave herself over to the pleasure that was waiting for her there, riding the tension he created inside her until it burst into a wave of heat and satisfaction.

Now she did pull away from him. She wanted him, still, but in a different way. Dakota moved backward so that he followed her up onto the bed, but only so she could have her way with him. She pushed him to the side when he tried to climb on top of her, pinning her knees on either side of his. Quickly stripping him of his clothes, Dakota ran her hands across the broad expanse of his tattooed chest and down his strong torso. Her palms explored the power of his thighs and the dark hairs scattered there, and she felt her nipples harden all over again as she bent forward to take his hard length into her mouth.

His body went taut, releasing slightly as he groaned when her hands and lips played over him. He brought his hands up to run them through her hair, bundling it into a rough ponytail so that it wouldn't obstruct his view. She slipped her tongue up his shaft and down again as she felt her excitement building for a second time.

Finally letting go and crawling forward, Dakota realized this was the first time in months that they'd truly been alone together and had the time to focus solely on each other. She relished his strong fingers on her hips and the way they grazed her thick backside as she guided him inside her. Their shared groan of relief made her smile. When she flicked her head back and happened to glance through the window at the endless expanse of countryside around them, she once again reveled in the knowledge of just how alone they were. Dakota braced herself against his shoulders as she rode him, pushing her body hard against his on the downward stroke to get exactly what she needed. He'd already primed her once, and it wasn't difficult to find that perfect point a second time. Here, she didn't have to be quiet. She could let the whole world know how much she enjoyed him. Dakota let out a cry of rapture as she gripped his shoulders.

He was there, too. Bryce pulled her down and crushed his lips against hers, his tongue plunging into her. One hand cradled her head and the other cupped a breast as his rhythm increased. Bryce pulled back and pressed his forehead to hers as he came, his fingers pressing into her flesh, reminding her of just how much she needed him.

Dakota rubbed her fingers delicately on his chest, watching the sun play on the ceiling as it worked its way down toward the horizon. She knew there was a wolf inside him, but it didn't bother her anymore. Whoever and whatever he was, she knew she wanted him. "Thank you."

He'd had his eyes closed, but he opened them as he rolled his head to the side and grinned at her. "I was that good, huh?"

"I meant for the house!" She playfully slapped his shoulder. "But yeah, that, too. I love you, Bryce."

"I love you, too. The house is really okay?"

She always smiled when she was near him, and that day, her cheeks were sore from it. Dakota sat up and flung the covers aside. "I love it. I can't wait to show the others."

"Soon." Bryce pulled her back down to him and kissed her forehead. "Let's have just a little more time together first."

"That sounds perfect." She settled into his arms and rested her head on his shoulder, excited for this new chapter they were about to begin.

THE END

If you enjoyed *Her Wrangler Wolf,* you'll love *Her Christmas Wolf,* the finale of the Wild Frontier Shifters series! Read on for a preview of Shaw's story.

SHAW

"I swear it comes earlier every year." Shaw frowned as he sat in the Full Moon Saloon's back office, glaring at the calendar. He pushed himself out of his chair and shoved through the door to the main area of the bar. It was a long and narrow space, but it would be packed with holiday shoppers within a few hours. "Hunter!"

"Right here, boss." A hand waved from behind the bar, and when Shaw got closer, he saw Hunter on the floor. "Just wiping down the shelves back here."

Shaw raised his eyebrows in surprise. It wasn't always easy to keep employees at a bar, even if he usually hired from within his own pack, but Hunter and his sister Savannah were working out quite well so far. "That'll have to wait. I need you to run out to the storage unit and get the Christmas decorations. Today's the damn Christmas Stroll."

"Already got 'em!" a cheerful voice announced from behind him.

Shaw turned to find Savannah walking in with a small cardboard box in her hands and confusion on her face. "This was all I could find, though."

"Yep. That's it. Can you get those put up in the windows for me?"

Savannah set the box on the bar and opened the top. "Seriously? This is it?" She pulled out a few sheets of very used, faded window clings, some tattered tinsel garland, and an old string of lights.

"I'm not much of a Christmas guy, but I'm not going to ruin it for everyone else." Shaw frowned at the small amount of décor, wishing he didn't have to put it up at all.

"I don't know. It might dampen their Christmas spirit when they see this," Savannah muttered as she peeled a battered gingerbread man cling off its backing.

Shaw ignored her. She didn't have to like the way he managed his bar. Considering the massive number of people who frequented the Full Moon

Saloon throughout the year, he obviously knew how to run the place.

"What are we doing for the buttons?" Hunter asked as he got up from the floor with his washrag.

"The buttons?"

"Yeah, you know. All the Christmas Stroll shoppers will be wearing those numbered buttons that they can use to win prizes and stuff. Our mom is always crazy about the Stroll, and we've been dragged along with her about a million times," Hunter explained.

"Oh, right." Shaw had forgotten about that part. "Let's see what we've got back here." He went behind the bar to take a peek at his stock of liquor bottles.

"A free shot?" Savannah asked from over near the front windows. "That's a great idea. That'll really bring them in. I could make a sign to put here in the window."

"If you'd like." Shaw's eyes expertly flicked through the inventory. He needed something that wasn't too expensive and wouldn't cost him a lot of overhead, but it had to be festive. He'd also need plenty of whatever he served because there would be a ton of people in there soon enough. "Here we go," he finally said as he set bottles of white crème de cacao and peppermint schnapps on the counter. "Chill these, and we'll make Polar Bear shots."

"Sounds good, boss!"

It didn't take long for the holiday fever to take over Sheridan. Main Street was completely shut down for four hours to kick off the Christmas season as shoppers took hay rides up and down the thoroughfare to shop, eat, and win prizes. There were plenty of them who also stopped into the Full Moon to get off their feet for a while and make the evening merry and bright as they eagerly claimed their free shots. There weren't as many tourists this time of year, but plenty of locals, including his buddies from his pack and other nearby clans.

"What the hell is *this*?" Wade said as he frowned at the shot glass of clear liquid. He and some of the other guys had stopped in while their mates were shopping.

"It's free," Colton replied as his ranch-roughened fingers closed around the tiny glass. "That's all I really need to know."

"Kinda girly if you ask me," Austin grumbled. It was a surprise to see him out at all since he mostly preferred to stay home at his ranch. No doubt his mate Harper, who was on the tourism board for

Sheridan, had dragged him out into public for a rare sighting.

"Oh, just suck it down and then we can get something a little more to our tastes," Cash advised. The deputy was off duty for the day, and he tipped his head back as he downed the shot. "That's a hangover waiting to happen."

Not to be outdone, the others joined him, each wincing over the minty-sweet flavor and the chill that went with it. Shaw gave them a one-sided smile and shrugged. "Chicks dig it."

The front door opened and allowed in another flood of people. Hunter and Savannah were busy checking on the tables and keeping the melted snow off the floor, so Shaw moved on down the bar.

But he nearly froze when his eyes landed on a woman who'd just settled down onto a stool near the corner. Her features were striking, with wide cheekbones and shining black hair. Her dark eyes danced as they watched him approach.

What caught Shaw's attention even more than her pretty face was the fact that he sensed an animal inside her. This in itself wasn't a surprise, considering how many shifters there were around those parts, but he didn't recognize her. She felt *different*.

His wolf was interested, too. Interested enough

that the normally calm beast was clawing to get out. He realized he was staring, and he grabbed the schnapps. "Take it you're here for your free shot?"

"If you're giving them away, I certainly won't turn one down. Besides, you look like you know what you're doing." Her eyes traveled down his arms and watched his hands as he expertly poured the liquor.

Shaw felt a shiver that sparked from her gaze and traveled straight up his arms and into his chest. She wasn't wearing a Christmas Stroll button like everyone else, but he pushed the drink toward her anyway. "It's called a Polar Bear shot."

Her fingers closed around the glass, but her eyes remained on his. One slim, dark eyebrow tweaked up a little as her chin tipped down, and he understood that they both knew each other's secret. "A Polar Bear shot. How very appropriate...for me." She tossed it back without any of the overreaction the guys had shown and set it down gently before leaning forward a little. "And what shot would describe yourself?"

"A Wolf Bite," he answered instantly, as his eyes settled on the side of her neck and he wondered just what it might be like to rake his teeth along it. Coming to his senses, Shaw cleared his throat and grabbed a rag to wipe the bar down. He'd made it a personal rule not to flirt with his customers, and he'd broken it big time. "I don't think I've seen you around here before. What brings you to Sheridan? Besides the drinks, of course."

"The drink was just a bonus," she said with a smile. "Actually, I'm here to see if you're hiring."

———

Beverly Hills Dragons Series

Dragons of Sin City Series

Dragons of the Darkblood Secret Society Series

Packs of the Pacific Northwest Series

Compilations

Forever Fated Mates Collection

Shifter Daddies Collection

Early Novellas

Mated By The Dragon Boss

Claimed By The Werebears of Green Tree

Bearer of Secrets

Rogue Wolf

ABOUT THE AUTHOR

Steamy shifter romance author Meg Ripley is a Seattle native who's relocated to New England. She can often be found whipping up her next tale curled up in a local coffee house with a cappuccino and her laptop.

Download *Alpha's Midlife Baby,* the steamy prequel to Meg's Fated Over Forty series, when you sign up for the Meg Ripley Insiders newsletter!

Sign up by visiting www.authormegripley.com

Connect with Meg

amazon.com/Meg-Ripley/e/B00Z8I9AXW
tiktok.com/@authormegripley
facebook.com/authormegripley
instagram.com/megripleybooks
bookbub.com/authors/meg-ripley
goodreads.com/megripley